DEAR READERS:

A few years ago, I wrote a book called *The Best Friend*. And hundreds of you wrote to tell me how unhappy you were with the ending. You thought Honey Perkins should pay for her crimes.

But I needed your help. I wasn't sure exactly what should happen to Honey. So we held a contest to let you decide. I got thousands of great ideas. It was hard to choose, but I finally picked my favorite. A girl named Sara Bikman from Grafton, Wisconsin, sent in the winning entry. Thanks, Sara!

So here is the book you've all been waiting for. Honey is back—and she's after Becka Norwood. But this time, Honey will get what she deserves. Won't she?

RL Stine

Books by R.L. Stine

Fear Street

THE NEW GIRL	THE MIND READER
THE SURPRISE PARTY	WRONG NUMBER 2
THE OVERNIGHT	TRUTH OR DARE
MISSING	DEAD END
THE WRONG NUMBER	FINAL GRADE
THE SLEEPWALKER	SWITCHED
HAUNTED	COLLEGE WEEKEND
HALLOWEEN PARTY	THE STEPSISTER 2
THE STEPSISTER	WHAT HOLLY HEARD
SKI WEEKEND	THE FACE
THE FIRE GAME	SECRET ADMIRER
LIGHTS OUT	THE PERFECT DATE
THE SECRET BEDROOM	THE CONFESSION
THE KNIFE	THE BOY NEXT DOOR
PROM QUEEN	NIGHT GAMES
FIRST DATE	RUNAWAY
THE BEST FRIEND	KILLER'S KISS
THE CHEATER	ALL-NIGHT PARTY
SUNBURN	THE RICH GIRL
THE NEW BOY	CAT
THE DARE	WHO KILLED THE
BAD DREAMS	HOMECOMING QUEEN?
DOUBLE DATE	INTO THE DARK
THE THRILL CLUB	THE BEST FRIEND 2
ONE EVIL SUMMER	

Available from ARCHWAY Paperbacks

THE
BEST
FRIEND 2

A Parachute Press Book

AN ARCHWAY PAPERBACK
Published by POCKET BOOKS
New York London Toronto Sydney Tokyo Singapore

This book is a work of fiction. Names, characters, places and incidents are products of the author's imagination or are used fictitiously. Any resemblance to actual events or locales or persons, living or dead, is entirely coincidental.

AN ARCHWAY PAPERBACK *Original*

 An Archway Paperback published by
POCKET BOOKS, a division of Simon & Schuster Inc.
1230 Avenue of the Americas, New York, NY 10020

Copyright © 1997 by Parachute Press, Inc.

ISBN: 0-671-52965-X

First Archway Paperback printing November 1997

10 9 8 7 6 5 4 3 2 1

FEAR STREET is a registered trademark of Parachute Press, Inc.

AN ARCHWAY PAPERBACK and colophon are registered trademarks of Simon & Schuster Inc.

Cover art by Bill Schmidt

Printed in the U.S.A.

IL 7+

part 1

chapter

1

 I stopped on the stone steps of the school building and took a deep breath. Two girls, humming a song together loudly and out-of-tune, pushed past me and entered the school.

My eyes stopped at the engraved sign beside the entrance: WAYNESBRIDGE HIGH SCHOOL. Someone had stuck a big wad of purple bubble gum on the W.

Becka Norwood, you're starting a whole new life, I told myself.

Waynesbridge was the next town from Shadyside, where I lived until this fall. But today it seemed a million miles away.

A new school. A new beginning.

That's what I kept repeating to myself all morning as I got dressed and walked the three blocks from my new house.

If only my heart would stop racing!

I'm not the calmest person in the world. Let's face it, I'm always a trembling mess in new situations. Mom used to say that I was *born* hyper. She said I learned to worry before I learned to walk!

When I was a freshman at Shadyside High, we had to write descriptions of ourselves for an English paper. I wrote that, for me, going through life was like walking high above the ground on a tightrope. I constantly had to struggle to keep my balance. And I always worried that the rope might snap in two and send me falling.

I got an A on the paper. But I also had to go see the school guidance counselor—Mr. Vincent with his annoying stutter and his bad breath.

Why am I thinking about that now? I asked myself. That's old news. Why am I standing in front of this new school, thinking about that old garbage?

I'd promised myself a thousand times to put those memories away. I had so many bad memories of Shadyside and my house on Fear Street. The memories felt like a two-ton weight on my chest, pressing me down, so heavy I couldn't breathe.

I shook out my long, auburn hair, trying to shake away those thoughts. Yes, I'd let my hair grow long again. And I'd lost a little weight. Just a few pounds. I was still what people call "full-figured."

I'm not exactly pretty. Or cute. But I'm okay.

And I'm starting to feel good about myself. I really am.

I shifted my backpack and prepared to go inside. I took another deep breath, hesitating. I stared at the wad of purple bubble gum again.

Something was holding me back. Keeping me at the school entrance. I knew what it was. I had one more hurdle to jump over.

One more guidance counselor. I had to see her first thing, before reporting to my homeroom.

What was her name again?

I'd written it on a scrap of paper. But where did I put it?

Two cheerleaders in their black-and-yellow uniforms passed by. One of them stopped outside the door to straighten her short, pleated skirt. She smiled at me, then hurried after her friend.

She looked a little like Trish, my friend back home. Except Trish was never a cheerleader.

"Go Hornets," I muttered. I found the slip of paper wadded up in my jacket pocket. Miss Englund. I hoped she wasn't totally uncool.

I had talked to so many counselors and doctors and shrinks in the past year. Most of them didn't have a clue.

I sighed and shoved the scrap of paper back in my pocket. I guess I can go through the story one more time, I decided. If it really does mean a brand-new start. A whole new Becka . . .

Miss Englund was young and kind of pretty. She had warm, brown eyes and a nice, friendly smile.

A lot of the counselors I'd met in the past year had nice, friendly smiles. I think they practiced them in the mirror before I came in. Maybe they took a Friendly Smile course in college.

She had a small office behind the main office. I saw a cluttered desk, two small green chairs across from it, and a table with a bottle of Evian water on it. The wall across from the window was covered with an old Marx Brothers movie poster.

She waved me to one of the green chairs and told me to call her Barbara. Then she shuffled through my file, frowning as she read over some things.

After a minute or so, she raised her dark eyes to me and got right down to business. "Becka—tell me about Honey Perkins," she said.

I let out a gasp. I guess I was expecting some easy questions first. But I got myself together pretty quickly.

I'm used to talking about Honey, after all.

I've been talking about her for months. Honey Perkins . . . the girl who ruined my life.

I rested my head on the seat back. I brushed a strand of my auburn hair off my forehead. "What do you want to know?" I asked.

Miss Englund leaned forward across her desk, studying me. "Start at the beginning," she said.

So I started at the beginning. I told her how Honey burst into my room one day while I was talking with Trish and Lilah. I told her how excited Honey acted, how she threw her arms around me, and hugged me, and said it was so good to see her old best friend again. And how she knew we'd be best, best friends from then on.

And I had no memory of this girl. I didn't think I'd ever seen her before. Trish and Lilah didn't remember her, either.

But there she was, taking over the conversation, ignoring my friends, gazing at me with her eyes all wild and lit up, as if I were the Crown Jewels or a big hunk of chocolate cake.

Weird.

But it got weirder.

After that day, I couldn't shake Honey. She kept popping up everywhere.

I found her in my room, trying on all the clothes in my closet. She borrowed things of mine and then never returned them. When I asked for them back, she insisted I gave them to her as a gift.

She and her father had moved next door, so she was constantly popping in at my house. She made me walk to school with her every morning. "Just like the old days," Honey said.

But I didn't remember any old days!

Then things started to get creepy. Honey cut her hair short and styled it to look exactly like mine. She started wearing the same clothes as me. She went out with my old boyfriend.

She was copying me, copying my life.

And when I complained, when I tried to stop her, she tried to *ruin* my life. First, she went after my *real* best friends.

Lilah was in a bad accident on her bike. Someone had messed up her brakes. She was in a coma for days. We didn't know if Lilah would live or not.

Then Honey pushed Trish down a flight of stairs. Broke her neck. I thought Trish was dead. I really did.

Honey swore it was an accident.

But I knew the truth.

Honey was trying to kill my friends so she could be my best friend.

After Trish was taken to the hospital, I totally lost it. It was just too terrifying. My mind just snapped.

Our family doctor sent me to bed. He said I needed a lot of quiet and a lot of rest.

But I didn't get it. Because the worst was still to come. Honey wasn't finished.

She killed my boyfriend. Bill Planter. That was his name.

Bill. Bill . . .

The only boy I ever really loved.

Honey killed him. Stabbed him in her kitchen. Then she put the knife in my hand. I had passed out or something.

I don't really remember. Could *you* remember something so horrible?

Honey murdered Bill—and made me believe that I had done it.

I stared at the knife. I stared at all the blood. And I believed her. I believed I was a murderer.

"I'm your best friend," Honey said to me as I stared at the river of blood on her kitchen floor. The blood on the knife . . . The blood on my hands . . .

"I'm your best friend," she repeated over and over. "I'll protect you, Becka, because I'm your best friend from now on. Your best friend."

I gazed up at Miss Englund. She was scribbling something on a long writing pad. My hands ached. I looked down and saw that I'd been squeezing the chair arms. My hands were cold and dripping wet.

"That's the story," I said weakly. I've told it a thousand times. But it upsets me each time. It turns my stomach into a hard, tight knot.

The guidance counselor scribbled for a few seconds more, chewing her bottom lip. Finally, she turned to me. "That was last winter," she said softly.

I nodded.

"Now you're ready for a fresh start?"

I nodded again. "I won't let Honey ruin my life," I told her. "I promised myself that."

"That's good," Miss Englund said. She forced a smile and stood up. "I know you will be okay, Becka," she assured me, straightening the bottom of her gray pullover sweater. "And I will be here to help you. You and I will talk often. Whenever you feel you need me. I want you to think of me as a friend."

I laughed. "My *best* friend?"

Her smile faded.

"Just joking," I said quickly.

"It . . . it's good that you can make jokes," she replied. "It's a very healthy sign." She leaned forward, pressing both hands on the desk. "You can do it," she assured me. "I know you can make a good new start here at Waynesbridge."

Then she stepped around the desk and shook my hand. I felt kind of awkward, especially since my hand was so cold and wet.

I knew she was trying to be nice. But I'd had it up to *here* with doctors and counselors trying to be nice. I just wanted to get on with my life.

I muttered thanks and made my way out the door. I passed through the principal's office where two parents were arguing with the secretary. "Where is the transcript?" the father was shouting. "How could you lose the stupid transcript?"

I stepped into the quiet of the main hall. First

period had begun. The hall was deserted except for a tall, lanky teacher leaning over a water fountain against the wall.

And then three boys came around the corner, walking quickly side by side, all three talking at once.

I started to turn away—but the boy in the middle caught my eye. Tall, athletic looking. And his face . . .

"No—!" I let out a high shriek that echoed down the hall.

My breath caught in my throat.

"Bill!" I cried. "I don't *believe* it! Bill! You're *alive!"*

chapter

2

Bill! Bill!

My shoes thudded on the hard floor as I hurtled toward him. Dove at him. Threw my arms around him.

"Bill!" I gasped out his name again and again. "Bill! Bill!" I pressed my face against his. So good to feel him. So good to feel the warmth of his skin.

Alive!

Bill!

He didn't move. He didn't respond. He stood still, stiff as a statue.

Sobbing, I pulled my face away. "Bill?"

Oh no. No . . .

Not Bill.

Tears flowed down my cheeks, my tears of joy. Too late to stop them as I stared into this stranger's face.

I could feel my face turning hot. I knew I was blushing. My knees trembled. I felt as if I might crumple to the floor.

Not Bill. Not Bill.

How many times had this happened to me in the past year? How many times had I imagined that I saw poor, dead Bill?

One day last summer I thought I saw him playing basketball on a playground with a bunch of guys. I ran across the court, broke up the game, threw my arms around him.

The boy was so embarrassed. He practically shoved me away. I could hear his friends teasing him as I hurried away. "Billy Boy. Hi, Billy Boy!" they were calling him.

I ran for blocks. I ran and ran, but I could still hear their cruel laughter in my ears.

And now, on my first day at Waynesbridge High, these three boys were laughing at me too.

"His name is Steve," one of them told me. And that got them laughing all over again.

I struggled to wipe the tears from my face. "You look like somebody," I managed to choke out.

"No, he doesn't!" one of the boys joked. "He doesn't look like anybody on this planet!"

"I'm sorry. Really," I said. My legs were feeling a little less wobbly. I turned and started to walk away.

"Hey—" the boy called after me. Not Bill. Not Bill.

I turned back to him. He didn't look like Bill at all. He was blond and had a chubby baby face with freckles on his nose.

How could I have thought he was Bill?

"Can we help you?" Steve asked. "You're new, right?"

"Yeah." My heart still pounded in my chest. I knew my face was still red.

I don't usually wear eye makeup. But I'd put some on this morning for my first day. Now I probably had black streaks running down my face.

"Do you know where you're going?" Steve asked.

The other two boys smirked. But I could tell that Steve was trying to be nice.

"Mr. Wright's room?" I asked. That was my first class. History of the European Peoples, I think it was called.

Steve pointed to the stairs at the end of the hall. "Go upstairs. It's the second door on the left."

I thanked him and started jogging to the stairs. Behind me, I could hear the boys laugh again. "Who's Bill?" I heard one of them ask.

Steve is a nice guy, I thought, making my way up the stairs. I practically tackled him. I made a total fool of myself. But he pretended as if everything was perfectly normal.

Normal.

What happened *was* perfectly normal, I told myself.

Becka, you were just talking about Bill to the counselor. And so you had Bill on your mind. That's all. No big deal.

I stopped in front of the second door on the left, smoothed my hair off my shoulders, and stepped inside. The class had begun. Kids sat quietly, leaning over open notebooks.

". . . Which brings us to the *real* cause of the war," Mr. Wright was saying. He sat on the front edge of his desk, his long legs crossed. He opened his mouth to begin his next sentence, but stopped when he noticed me.

I walked slowly along the chalkboard to the front of the room. I could see everyone turn to look at me. I hoped they couldn't see the tear stains on my cheeks or my smeared eye makeup.

Mr. Wright climbed to his feet as I approached. He was tall and broad-shouldered. He had thinning black hair and wore large, black-rimmed eyeglasses. He wore a gray sweater, torn at one shoulder, over black corduroy slacks. As I walked closer, I could see a hearing aid in his right ear.

"Are you Becka?" he asked, scratching his balding forehead.

I nodded. "Yes. Sorry, I'm late."

"Well, you're about three weeks late," he replied, frowning.

"I just moved here," I told him.

"You'll catch up," he said, his expression softening. "Borrow the notes from somebody, and you'll be okay." He turned to the class. "This is Becka . . . ?"

"Norwood," I said.

"Becka Norwood," the teacher repeated.

They all stared at me. A few kids muttered hi. It was kind of awkward.

"Do you know anyone in here?" Mr. Wright asked me.

I shook my head. "No. Not really."

"I'm sure you'll help Becka feel at home," he told the class. He spoke very loudly. I guessed maybe his hearing aid didn't work that well.

A few kids muttered hello as I walked to the back of the room to take a seat at the only free desk. I dropped my backpack to the floor and slipped into the chair.

Mr. Wright had returned to his perch on the front of his desk and had resumed his lecture. "You cannot always believe the history books on this subject," he was saying.

What's the subject? I wondered.

I suddenly felt lost. This was like coming in in the middle of a movie and not having a clue who anybody is or what has happened so far.

"Hi. I'm Glynis Quinn," the red-haired girl next to me leaned close and whispered. She had bright green eyes and full red lips. She was pretty awesome looking. I mean, she looked like a model.

"Better take notes," she whispered.

"Huh?" I wasn't sure what she was saying.

"The Germans had a three-pronged public relations program," Mr. Wright was saying. "The idea was to keep their *real* intentions from public scrutiny."

Wow. This is a tough course, I thought. Do the other kids understand what he is saying?

"Take really good notes," Glynis repeated. "All the tests come from the notes."

I nodded and reached into my backpack for a notebook.

Glynis kept her eyes on me. "Just write down everything he says," she whispered. "That's the easiest way."

"Thanks," I murmured. I pulled a pen from the outside pocket of the backpack and opened my notebook to the first page.

"The question is," Mr. Wright was saying, "how long can you fool the governments of the world? How long can you keep them in the dark?"

I glanced around the room. Everyone was silently hunched over notebooks, writing down every word. A girl near the window hiccupped. No one giggled or laughed. Everyone kept writing.

I settled into the seat and began to take notes. After a short while, I realized that Mr. Wright was discussing the causes of World War II.

I followed Glynis's instructions and wrote down almost every word he said. When Mr. Wright took a short break for a drink of water, I turned to Glynis. "Thanks for the tip," I said.

She smiled. She had a beautiful smile. It made her green eyes light up. "He lectures every day," she told me. "He never asks us any questions or anything. We never discuss anything. He just lectures."

"Weird," I replied. Then I added, "I like your nails." She had great, glossy brown fingernails.

"Chocolate," she replied, holding up both hands so I could see better. "That's the flavor of the week." She laughed.

I hid my hands from her. I didn't want her to see my chewed, broken nails.

Mr. Wright set down his bottle of water and

began pacing back and forth in front of the chalk-board. Closing his eyes, he began his lecture again.

I bent over my notebook and began to write. I couldn't really concentrate on what he was saying. I had to write too fast.

But I had to admit to myself that it felt good to be back in school, doing classwork like a normal high school student. Sure, I felt nervous. But I felt happy too, and excited.

I glanced around the room at all the unfamiliar faces. Maybe there are some new friends in here for me, I told myself. Maybe I'm going to meet some terrific new kids.

Maybe I'll meet a *real* best friend.

And then I can forget about Honey forever.

I glanced at Glynis. Then I shut out all other thoughts and listened to Mr. Wright's lecture, writing, writing as fast as I could.

When the bell rang, the others all snapped their notebooks shut. Mr. Wright stopped talking instantly and made a grab for his water bottle.

Chairs scraped. Kids started talking and laughing and heading to their next class.

I started to say something to Glynis, but she was walking out the door with another girl. I checked my schedule to see where to go next.

Then I gazed down at my open notebook—and gasped.

I squinted at the page. Squinted harder.

No! I thought. *No! Please—I didn't do that! Please—tell me that I didn't do that!*

But no matter how long or hard I stared at the page, the words wouldn't go away.

BILL. BILL. BILL. BILL.

To my horror, I saw that I had written his name—BILL. BILL. BILL. BILL. BILL—over and over, page after page.

BILL. BILL. BILL . . .

chapter 3

"How was your first day?"

I turned from my locker to see Glynis standing beside me. "Not bad, I guess," I replied, kicking some books back against the locker wall. School had just ended, and I was trying to decide what to take home and what to leave.

Glynis laughed at my attempts to get stuff to stay in the locker. She had a deep, throaty laugh. Very sexy. "They make the lockers just about big enough to hold a pencil," she joked.

I couldn't help staring at her. She was so pretty. She reminded me a lot of that actress, Claire Danes. She wore a yellow vest over a white T-shirt and had a short green skirt over brown tights. Very slim and trim. I felt like a cow standing next to her.

"I can't imagine changing schools senior year," she said, shifting her backpack. "I mean, how tough is that?"

I shrugged. "I'm kind of psyched for it," I confessed. "I hated my old school."

"Where did you go?" she asked.

"Shadyside," I answered. I really didn't want to talk much about Shadyside. I hoped Glynis didn't remember the story about me and Honey and Bill. It was on the news and in the papers.

I wanted a clean start in Waynesbridge. I didn't want kids pointing at me when I walked by and gossiping about me.

Glynis brushed back her red hair, and I saw the chocolate fingernails again. "I did licorice nail polish once," I told her, "but my dad said I looked like a witch."

Glynis laughed and started to say something. But a tall, lanky boy with his hair pulled back in a blond ponytail came up behind her and playfully bumped her against the wall of lockers.

"Hey—Frankie!" she cried, regaining her balance. "Give me a break!"

"What's up, Glyn?" he asked. He was nearly a head taller than us. He wore a red-and-black flannel shirt open over a red T-shirt and shabby, faded jeans torn at both knees. He had silvery gray eyes and a great smile.

She reached up and tugged hard at his ponytail, pulling his head back, tugging until he cried out. "Stop bumping me," she ordered him. "Pick on someone your own size."

I slammed my locker shut and fiddled with the straps on my backpack. I think Glynis had forgotten I was still there. "Guess I'll go home," I said.

"Oh. Hey. This is Becka," Glynis told Frankie. "She just started today."

Frankie studied me for a moment. "The new girl," he said, smiling. His silvery eyes twinkled when he smiled. "You're in my bio lab fifth period."

"Yeah. Right," I replied. I suddenly remembered seeing him in the first row of lab tables.

"You like to cut up animals?" he asked.

Like Bill? I thought.

I pictured the knife in my hand. All the blood . . .

"I don't know," I answered. "I've never tried it."

"So how do you like Waynesbridge so far?" he asked. "It sucks—right?"

Glynis gave him a hard shove. "Give her a break, Frankie. What's she supposed to say after one day?"

"It's okay so far," I told him.

I think he likes me, I decided. He keeps smiling at me and giving me the eye, as if he likes what he sees.

Glynis wrapped an arm around his waist. I could see they were real comfortable with each other. I guessed they'd been going together for a long time.

"Are we going to get a Coke or not?" Glynis asked. "I've got tons of homework."

"Yeah. Sure," Frankie replied, his eyes still on me. "I have homework, too, you know," he told Glynis with a sneer. "And I'm giving two guitar lessons tonight."

"You play guitar?" I asked him.

He nodded. "Yeah. Some guys and I have a band. And I give lessons. You know. To kids. It's pretty good money."

"Think you could teach me to play guitar?" I asked.

"Well . . ." To my surprise, he reached out and took my hand. His hand felt warm and strong. I felt a chill at the back of my neck.

He raised my hand close to his face and studied my fingers. "Well, Becka, you've got the nails for a guitar player," he said seriously.

I pulled my hand away. "What do you mean?" I snapped. I thought he was making fun of my chewed-up fingernails.

"You have to trim your nails real close to play," he replied. He held up his right hand. "Check it out. No nails." He held up Glynis's hand with the long, chocolate nails. "See? This girl cannot play guitar."

Glynis made a disgusted face. "I'm tone deaf anyway," she muttered. "My dad says I can't carry a tune in a bucket." She nudged Frankie. "Let's go." She started to push him down the hall.

He turned back to me. "Becka, want to come? We're just going to get Cokes and some pizza."

He *does* like me, I decided. I glanced at Glynis to make sure it was okay with her. Then I replied, "Sure. Thanks."

I tried to sound casual. But I really could feel something going on between Frankie and me. I wondered if Glynis noticed it too.

We walked two blocks to a little red and white restaurant called Pizzaz. It was already crowded with kids from school. Glynis and Frankie squeezed into one side of a booth in back, and I slid in across from them.

My knee bumped Frankie's under the table. I

waited for him to pull his knee away, but he didn't. He and Glynis were arguing about something that had happened last weekend. I slid closer to the wall.

We ordered a pizza and some Cokes. They stopped their argument and started to gossip about some kids in the front booth. I raised my eyes to the front. The boy and girl were holding hands across the table.

The door to the restaurant swung open. A boy in a leather bomber jacket stepped in.

It took me a few seconds to recognize him.

And then I jumped up and screamed, "I don't *believe* it!"

chapter

4

Glynis and Frankie cried out in surprise as I leaped out of the booth. I dodged past a waitress carrying two pizza trays, one in each hand. And ran breathlessly to the front of the restaurant.

"Eric!" I cried. "Eric! What are *you* doing here? I don't believe it!"

"Hey—" he said uncertainly. He squinted at me, confused. And then he forced a smile to his face. "Hey—hi. How's it going?"

"Great!" I exclaimed. I was so happy to see someone I knew. I hugged him and pressed my cheek against his.

Back in Shadyside, Eric and I had gone together for a few months—before Bill and I got together. I always liked Eric's dark eyes, his sense of humor. He could always make me laugh.

I guess I hugged him a little too long or something. His face turned a deep red and he pulled away from me. "Hey," he said. "You dumped me— remember?"

I gasped, startled by his bitterness.

I never realized I had really hurt him.

"I—I've changed," I managed to choke out. "I'm different now, Eric. I'm starting all over."

I realized I was gripping his arm.

He eyed me suspiciously. "You live here now?"

I nodded.

"You go to Waynesbridge?"

I nodded again. "Today was my first day." I motioned to the back booth. "I'm here with some new friends. Do you want to join us?"

He glanced at Glynis and Frankie. "Uh . . . no. I've got to go," he said. "I just drove over here to look for someone, but I—"

"You have your car?" I asked. "Want to drive around? We could talk. It would be like old times." I squeezed his arm again. I really did feel happy to see him. Actually, I was surprised by how happy I felt.

"Well . . ." He hesitated.

I waved to Glynis and Frankie. "Got to run!" I called. "See you tomorrow!"

They were busy talking. They both waved good- bye without interrupting their conversation.

I practically pulled Eric to his car, a little black Civic. I lowered myself into the passenger seat. My heart was pounding. All my good feelings for him flooded back.

When he climbed behind the wheel, I threw my arms around his neck. I pulled his face to mine. And I kissed him.

A long, lingering kiss filled with emotion.

When the kiss finally ended, Eric gazed at me, breathing hard. "Wow," he murmured. "You really *are* different!"

I kissed him again.

"Eric," I whispered. "Eric . . . Eric . . ."

I don't know how long we sat there in his little car, kissing and holding on to each other. I completely lost track of time.

Eric asked me to go to a movie or something with him Saturday night. I said that would be great.

Then I started kissing him again.

But as I pressed my lips harder against his mouth, I found myself thinking of Frankie.

Frankie . . .

He's so cute, I thought, with that blond ponytail, those silvery eyes.

I think Frankie really likes me, I told myself. I really think he likes me.

I broke our kiss. I leaned back against the seat, breathing hard.

"I've got to run," I told Eric. He looked so funny. I had smeared my lipstick all over his cheek.

He turned to the wheel and pushed back his dark hair with a sigh. "Can I drop you anywhere?" he asked. "Drive you home or something?"

I shook my head. "No thanks. See you Saturday." I pushed open the passenger door and slid out. I slammed the door shut. Then I ran off without looking back.

How weird running into Eric today, I thought, crossing the street and heading for home. The first day of my new life, and I run into my old boyfriend.

I guess you never can escape entirely from your old life.

I was glad to see Eric. I liked him a lot when I was back at Shadyside High. I always felt a little guilty for dumping him.

Eric is okay, I thought, turning the corner onto my block. He isn't as cool as Frankie. But it might be okay to spend some time with him again.

My head was practically exploding from all that had happened today. A new school. New classes and teachers. New friends . . . Eric and Frankie.

As soon as I got home, I hurried up to my room. I dropped my backpack on the floor. Then I stood in front of my dresser mirror and studied myself.

I pulled my hair straight back with both hands. I realized that my blond hair was only a few shades darker than Glynis's. And it was about the same length.

I gazed at myself, pulling my hair back, first over the right shoulder, then over the left. I'll straighten it out tonight, I decided.

I studied my fingernails. I had chewed them to the quick. But I could stop that bad habit, I told myself. I could let them grow.

Tomorrow, I'll buy that chocolate shade of nail polish that Glynis wears, I decided. It looks so cool.

With my hair straighter and pulled back, I look a lot like Glynis.

I wonder if Frankie will like that . . .

chapter
5

*T*he next day after school, I hurried to the mall and bought the chocolate nail polish. Back in my room, I carefully applied the thick, brown liquid. Then I admired my cool new nails as they dried.

Not bad, I decided. I checked out my new hairstyle in the mirror.

"All right!" I cheered myself. "Becka, you're looking good, girl!"

I picked up the phone to call Glynis. She promised I could borrow her history notes to help me catch up. And I wanted to tell her about my chocolate nails.

I handled the phone carefully because my nails were still wet. As I lifted the phone to my ear, I heard a voice on the line. "Hello? Hello?"

I recognized his voice instantly. "Frankie?"

"Hi, Becka," he said. "You busy or something?"

"No," I replied. "Just fooling around. What's up?"

There was a long pause. Then Frankie said, "I guess you saw me looking at you yesterday."

"Well . . ." My heart started pounding. I didn't know what to say.

"And I think you were checking me out too," Frankie continued.

A short, nervous laugh escaped my throat. I pressed the phone tighter to my ear. "Maybe I was," I teased.

"Well . . ." Frankie hesitated again. "It's kind of hard to say, Becka. But when I met you, I just . . . felt something, I guess. Like a flash."

I took a deep breath. "Frankie, I felt the same thing," I confessed.

"I just knew that you were someone special," Frankie continued, talking rapidly, excitedly. "In the restaurant, I kept wishing Glynis would go away so that we could be together."

"I . . ." My words caught in my throat. I felt so happy. So thrilled.

And then I realized that I was fantasizing the entire conversation. Frankie wasn't on the phone. I was making the whole thing up in my mind.

I uttered a gasp and tossed the phone onto my bed as if it were steaming hot.

"No . . . no . . ." I murmured. "Becka, get it together."

I started to pace back and forth.

You're acting crazy, I scolded myself. Becka, you're acting like Honey.

Crazy like Honey.

Imagining phone calls. Fantasizing a whole conversation.

It's okay to do that in your head. But it's not okay to really believe you're hearing Frankie's voice. It's not okay to talk into the phone when there's *no one* on the other end of the line!

I took a deep breath and held it. I started to feel a little calmer.

Okay, okay, I told myself. No harm done.

Everyone gets a little carried away, a little crazy, now and then. It's not as if I'm turning into Honey.

Honey . . .

Thinking about her brought a horrifying memory from last winter sweeping back into my mind. Once again, I was at my friend Trish's Christmas party. Once again, Honey crashed the party uninvited.

I turned to see her enter the room—and gasped. Honey had my short hairdo. And her outfit was identical to mine. The same short silver skirt over the same black catsuit.

I shuddered as I remembered Honey's first words to me that night at Trish's party. "Hiya, *twin.*"

That's what she said to me.

I stared at her openmouthed. Stared at my mirror image. Honey didn't want to be my best friend. She wanted to be *me!*

I saw girls pointing at us. A couple of kids laughed at me. Laughed at me because I suddenly had a twin.

I couldn't take it anymore. I screamed at her, "Honey—go away! Go away!"

I saw the hurt expression on her face. She turned

and ran, ran across Trish's living room and up the stairs.

A moment later, I saw Trish at the top of the stairs. She was carrying a huge Christmas yule log cake on a silver tray.

I saw Trish take a step.

And then I saw Honey at the top of the stairs, right behind Trish.

Trish took another step.

And then the chocolate-covered cake flew off the silver tray.

And Trish flew too.

She flew headfirst down the steep stairway.

She screamed all the way down. A sound I still hear when I'm lying in bed at night. A sound I'll never forget. A horrifying scream as she plunged down the stairs.

The tray hit first, clattering on the floor. Then Trish landed with a sickening *crack*.

And didn't move.

I remember raising my eyes to Honey at the top of the stairs. I remember the strange expression on Honey's face.

And I knew. I knew that Honey had pushed Trish.

Honey pushed my best friend Trish down the stairs to pay me back for yelling at her. And because Honey wanted to get rid of all my friends. She wanted to be my best friend, my *only* friend.

If she couldn't be my best friend, Honey would ruin my life.

She nearly did that night. Honey nearly ruined my life last winter.

She murdered Bill. She stabbed him and put the knife in my hand.

She murdered poor Bill. Poor, sweet Bill.

Honey tried to ruin my life. Honey tried everything to ruin my life.

But that was last year, I told myself, still pacing back and forth, my hands out at my sides so the nail polish would dry. That was last year. In a different place.

Honey isn't here now. Honey can't get me now.

"Stop thinking about her, Becka," I ordered myself out loud.

I blew on my chocolate nails. They were dry.

I stepped to the dresser mirror to check out my new look.

"Oh noooo." A low moan escaped my throat when I saw what I had done.

I stared in shock at my forehead. My cheeks. My chin.

At the name BILL . . . BILL . . . BILL. . . . Scrawled in brown nail polish all over my face.

chapter
_____

6

"*I*'m doing so much better," I told Miss Englund. "I'm just so happy about the way things are going."

I glanced up at the clock over her desk. Nearly four o'clock. I'd promised Glynis I'd come over right after school, and now I was very late.

Did I really need to stop by the guidance counselor's office for a friendly chat and progress report?

I don't think so.

I had my long heart-to-heart with her on Monday. And today was only Thursday.

But she had nabbed me in the hall as I was about to leave. She acted so surprised to see me, as if she hadn't been waiting there for me all along.

"Becka, do you have five minutes?" she asked so pleasantly. "I really would like to see how it's going with you. Just a short chat?"

"Do I have a choice?" That's what I wanted to say. But of course I didn't. Because I'm a polite person. And I wanted to stay on her good side.

She was only trying to be nice, after all.

So I followed Miss Englund to her little office behind the main office. We chatted about the assembly that afternoon. A dance troupe from Canada performed in the auditorium. Believe it or not, they tap-danced to classical music.

Glynis told me we have arts assemblies once a month. She said they're usually even weirder than this one. No one really cares what they are, though. Everyone is happy because the assemblies get us out of class.

"I thought they were very good. But I'm not sure why," Miss Englund said brightly, closing her office door behind me. "I mean, do we really *need* people tap-dancing to Bach?"

"I thought it was kind of dumb," I confessed, dropping into the chair across from her desk. "But the music was pretty."

She leaned across the cluttered desk, studying me as she had on Monday. "It's going okay?" she asked.

I shoved my hands into my jeans pockets and slumped lower in the seat. "Sure." I glanced at the clock again. I really wanted to get to Glynis's house.

"How are your classes?" the guidance counselor asked.

"Good," I replied.

She waited for me to continue. But I couldn't think of anything more to say. Finally, I added, "Really good."

"Do you feel that you are too far behind in any of them?" Miss Englund asked. "It must be a little hard starting school three weeks late."

I shook my head. "Well . . ." I hesitated. "I don't have all the notes from Mr. Wright's lectures. But Glynis is helping me. She's lending me her notes."

Miss Englund tapped her pencil eraser on top of the telephone. "You've made some friends?" she asked.

I glanced at the clock again. "Yeah," I grunted.

She gazed at me, waiting for me to say more.

I shifted uncomfortably on the leather chair. "I've made some friends," I told her. "Do you know Glynis Quinn? She's been really great to me."

The counselor nodded. "Yes. Glynis is a nice girl."

"Mainly, I've been feeling really happy," I told her. "I don't imagine that I see Bill everywhere I go. And I hardly think about Honey at all."

"Good," Miss Englund said softly, writing a short note on her pad.

"I feel as if I've really turned a corner," I said. "It's like I'm heading in the right direction now."

She scribbled a few more words on the pad, then raised her eyes to me. "Becka, you've changed your look. I really like your hair."

I laughed. "It's the new me!" I declared. "You know what, Miss Englund? I'm really starting to feel good about myself again."

I found Glynis's house on Broadmoor Drive, a big, white-shingled house surrounded by tall hedges and big flower gardens on both sides. The houses in this part of Waynesbridge all looked like mansions to me!

Glynis's room was about the size of my whole house. And she had a walk-in closet for her clothes as big as my bedroom.

We chatted about school for a while. Then she got a phone call from Frankie. As she talked in hushed tones, sprawling on her back on the bed, I explored her closet.

I pulled out a skirt and top I just couldn't resist. Glynis was chatting away, so I slid out of my clothes and tried on her outfit.

She was a little bit slimmer than me, I discovered. The skirt was tight at the waist. But if I lost a few pounds, her clothes would fit me easily.

I tried on another skirt and a couple of sweaters. I stepped up to the full-length mirror on the closet door to see how I looked.

"Not bad," Glynis said.

I turned to find her right behind me. I hadn't heard her get off the phone.

She pulled a sweater off the shelf. "Try this, Becka. It goes better with the skirt, I think. I bought them to go together."

"You have great clothes," I told her, taking the cream-colored sweater. It felt so soft. My sweaters are always scratchy.

"We'll have to go shopping soon," Glynis said, watching me as I pulled the sweater over my head. "I've really been in the mood."

"Me too," I replied. "Where do you like to shop?"

"Sometimes I go to those trendy little shops on

Harbor Drive," Glynis said. "But I usually drive to Shadyside and go to the mall."

I tugged down the sleeves of the sweater, brushed back my hair, and stepped to the mirror. Before I could admire myself, Glynis's mom strolled into the room.

She stopped in front of the doorway, and her mouth dropped open. "Wow! You two really look like twins!" she exclaimed.

Glynis turned to me and stared as if seeing me for the first time. "It's true, Becka! All of a sudden, we look so much alike!"

Glynis burst out laughing.

I could feel my face turn hot. Why was she laughing like that? I felt really hurt.

"What's funny about it?" I cried. "We're friends—aren't we?"

Glynis had to go downstairs to help her mom hang a new poster in the den. I quickly changed back into my clothes. Then I folded Glynis's skirt and sweater carefully and tucked them into my backpack.

I knew Glynis wouldn't mind if I borrowed them.

Why should she mind?

Best friends always borrow each other's clothes.

That's what best friends do.

chapter

7

I planned to wear Glynis's outfit on Saturday night when I went out with Eric. But the weather turned much warmer—Indian summer—so I had to find something else.

On Friday night, when Glynis invited me to come shopping with her and Frankie, I jumped at the chance.

I waited for them on the corner near my house. It was a hot, humid night. No breeze. No air at all. It felt more like summer than fall.

I checked my watch. They were late. I sat down on the curb and leaned back on my hands. I gazed up at a clear sky filled with twinkling stars.

I took a deep breath. I suddenly felt so happy.

New friends. A new me.

The honk of a car horn shook me from my thoughts. I turned to see Frankie's Jeep right in front of me. "Becka—let's go!" he called. "Let's *move!*" He revved the engine.

I climbed into the backseat. Glynis turned and smiled at me from the front. "We're going to check out the Division Street Mall," she announced.

"Sounds good," I replied, struggling with the seat belt. I could see Frankie eyeing me in the rearview mirror. Once again, I felt a flash—a special closeness between Frankie and me.

"Uh . . . Becka?" Glynis started reluctantly. She had turned and was staring straight ahead as Frankie moved the Jeep onto the expressway to Shadyside. "Did you . . . borrow my skirt and sweater yesterday afternoon?"

I finally clicked the seat belt. "Yes," I told her. "Do you need them back right away?"

Silence for a few seconds. Then Glynis replied, "No. Not right away."

"I'm going out tomorrow night with a guy I used to know," I told her. "I thought maybe I'd wear your stuff. But it's way too warm."

"Well, just return them when you have a chance," Glynis said, glancing at Frankie.

"No problem," I replied.

The Division Street Mall was always crowded on Friday nights. Frankie had to drive around the front parking lot twice before he found a place, about a mile from the stores.

As we walked to the entrance, I wondered if I would run into any of my old friends from Shadyside High. I suddenly felt tense. My hands were ice cold. I realized I didn't want to see anyone I used to know.

Becka, you're a new person, I told myself. If you do run into someone from your old life, it won't matter. Because they're in the past. You're in the present.

No. You're in the future. You're in your *new* future.

We started at The Clothes Hangar, a huge store that carries designer brands at a big discount. I walked around a bit. Then I began pawing through some faded jeans piled on a table, searching for my size.

I found a pair near the bottom of the pile. When I pulled it out, a whole stack of jeans toppled to the floor. With a groan, I bent to pick them up.

Someone bent down to help me. A dark-haired boy.

I raised my eyes to him—and cried out.

"Huh? *Eric?*"

His mouth dropped open in surprise.

"What are *you* doing here?" we both cried out at once.

Then we both laughed. I stood up with an armful of jeans and dropped them back on the table.

"Do you *work* here?" I asked, still stunned.

"Yeah," Eric replied. "Friday nights and all day Saturday. You know. I do stock and stuff. It pays pretty well. My uncle got me the job."

I held up the jeans in my size. "Do you get a store discount?"

He frowned. "Not really." He narrowed his dark eyes at me. "What are you doing in the old neighborhood?"

"I still come here to shop sometimes," I told him. "Most of the stores in Waynesbridge are so tacky. And the only good ones are way too expensive for me."

Eric started to reply. But Glynis and Frankie walked over to me. I introduced them to Eric.

"I've seen you before, I think," Eric told Frankie. "Are you on the Hornets' basketball team?"

Frankie laughed. "No way. Just because I'm tall doesn't mean I can play basketball. I'm a total klutz."

Glynis tugged Frankie's ponytail. "Come on. I'm suddenly *starving!*"

Frankie turned to me. "Glyn and I are going to the food court, Becka. Want to come?"

"I'll catch up with you," I replied. "I want to talk to Eric. And I want to look around here some more."

Glynis pulled Frankie by the hand. "Come *on!*" she called back to me. "We'll wait for you down there, Becka. See you!"

I watched her pull Frankie away. At the exit, Frankie turned back to me and shrugged. Then they disappeared.

When I turned back to Eric, his expression had changed. He stared at me suspiciously. "Why did they call you Becka?" he demanded.

I stared back at him. "Excuse me?"

"You heard me, Honey," Eric insisted. "Those two kids—why did they call you Becka?"

He grabbed my arm. "Did you tell them your name was Becka?" he asked heatedly. "Honey— are you pretending to be Becka? What's going on?"

chapter

8

"Let go of my arm!" I cried. "You're *hurting* me!"

Eric released me and stepped back. "Stop shouting," he whispered. "I'm working—remember?"

Over his shoulder, I saw a sales clerk behind the cash register staring at us.

"Honey," Eric whispered breathlessly. "What are you doing? Did you tell those kids you were Becka Norwood?"

My heart pounded. I suddenly felt so angry. Furious! I wanted to hit him. To pound him. I wanted to tear Eric apart!

"I *am* Becka now!" I screamed.

"Sshhhh!" he hissed. He grabbed my shoulders with both hands and backed me up, into the narrow doorway that led to the dressing rooms. "Honey—" he started.

"Don't call me that!" I shrieked. I couldn't help

it. I couldn't keep quiet. I couldn't stand there and let him ruin my new life.

"I'm Becka now!" I insisted. "I'm not Honey anymore! I'm Becka! I'm Becka!"

I shoved his hands off my shoulders. I stormed away from the dressing rooms.

I could feel the blood pulsing at my temples. I had throbbing pains behind my eyes. Everything kept flashing red. Bright red.

I spun around to face Eric.

"I'm Becka now!" I told him, spitting the words furiously in his face. "Honey doesn't exist anymore. I left her behind. I left her in the past."

He stared at me, his eyes wide with confusion—with fear.

"I'm all new!" I cried. "I started a whole new life. I'm a whole new person. I'm not Honey anymore, Eric. I'm Becka now—and you're not going to ruin it! No way I'm going to let you ruin it!"

I grabbed him.

I don't know what I planned to do.

I was out of control. I couldn't think clearly. I couldn't think at all.

The pain throbbed behind my eyes. At my temples.

The room tilted. I saw everything through bright flashes of red.

Two women with shopping bags stopped talking to stare at me. Behind them, the store clerk gaped at us sternly.

But I didn't care. I didn't care who saw me.

I had to protect my new name. I had to protect my new life.

I couldn't let Eric call me Honey. I couldn't let him tell my new friends who I was.

"Honey, please—" he begged quietly, his eyes on the store clerk. "Let go."

"I'm Becka!" I shrieked. "I'm Becka! Becka!"

"But, you can't be!" he cried in a trembling voice. He jerked free of my grasp. And then he pointed behind me.

"You can't be Becka," he declared, turning me around. "Because there's the *real* Becka—right there!"

I spun away from him. And squinted through the flashing red.

And saw her.

Saw her. Saw her.

Becka Norwood.

Becka Norwood, staring in horror at me from the next aisle.

And that's when I lost it.

"Noooooo!"

An animal wail escaped my throat.

"I'm Becka! I'm Becka!" I cried furiously, in a shrill screech of a voice I'd never heard before. "This is a trick! But you can't fool me! I'm Becka now!"

The pain throbbed in my head.

I stared at Becka, who was gaping back at me.

I had to shut my eyes. I had to make her disappear.

But when I opened them, she was still there.

"Honey—" Eric said softly, reaching for me.

"No! No!" I cried.

I couldn't let them ruin my new life. I couldn't let the two of them play this cruel trick on me.

"No! Noooooooooo!"

Frantically, gasping for breath, I grabbed something off the glass countertop. Something heavy.

45

Beads?

Yes. A long rope of heavy, glass beads.

Eric reached again for me. But I was too fast.

I held the heavy beads in both hands—and pulled them down over his head.

"No! No! Nooooooo!" Were those shrill, animal cries coming from me?

I tightened the beads around Eric's throat.

Pulled. Pulled . . .

"You're not going to spoil it!" I told him through gritted teeth. "No way! No way you can spoil it!"

I pulled the beads tighter, wrapping them, wrapping them around his throat.

He uttered a gasp. His hands shot up to his neck.

But I held on, tightening the beads, pulling them tighter . . . tighter.

I saw the glass cut into his skin.

Drops of bright red blood trickled onto the glass.

"Honey—" he choked out.

"Noooooo!" I moaned. "Not Honey! Not Honey!"

I tightened the rope of beads. The glass dug into his throat. His face darkened to red.

Then purple.

He was on his knees now, gasping and choking. His eyes bulged wide with fright.

His hands tore at the beads.

But I was too strong. Too strong. My *fury* made me strong.

Blood flowed over the beads, down his neck.

He uttered a final gasp. Then his eyes shut and he dropped heavily to the floor.

I didn't let go. I tightened the beads. Wrapped them tighter . . . wrapped them.

I didn't let go until I felt hands on my shoulders. Hands grabbing me roughly, pulling me away.

I spun around and saw Becka. She had me by the shoulders. She pulled me with all her strength.

"Let go! Let go!" she cried.

But then she stopped.

I staggered back, the blood-soaked beads in my hand. And saw her staring down, staring down at Eric's body, sprawled on the floor, his face bright purple, blood gushing from his neck.

"You—you *killed* him!" Becka gasped.

chapter

10

"No! *You* did it!" I choked out.

My whole body trembled and shook. I was panting hard, my chest heaving up and down.

"You did it, Becka!" I repeated.

I raised my hand gripping the beads. Blood smeared over my palm.

So much blood. Eric's blood.

"Unnnnh." I uttered a sick cry—and tossed the beads to Becka.

Stunned, she caught them in both hands.

"You killed Eric, Becka!" I told her. "And I'll pay you back!"

I was trembling so hard, I could barely control myself.

"I'll pay you back!" I shrieked at her. "You murdered Bill. And now you've murdered my new life!"

I saw the store clerk coming. Coming fast.

He lowered his shoulder to tackle me.

He grabbed one leg. But I scrambled free.

And ran for the door.

"Get her! Stop her!" he cried.

I heard cries of surprise and horrified screams.

I ducked down an aisle of denim jackets, then spun through another aisle, shooting toward the door.

As I reached the exit, I could see Becka reflected in the glass.

She hadn't moved. She stood over Eric's body, the blood-soaked beads gripped in her hand.

I burst through the doorway—and saw two grim-faced police officers running toward the store.

"Stop her!" I called to them. I pointed frantically to Becka. "She killed him! Stop her!"

chapter

11

My two best friends, Trish Walters and Lilah Brewer, came to Eric's funeral with me. It was held on a gray, rainy Monday morning in the little church three blocks from our school, Shadyside High.

The three of us sat in the back row and stared straight ahead as the minister performed the ceremony. I wrapped my jacket around me. It felt about twenty degrees colder in the church, and very damp.

In the front pew, Eric's mother and father were weeping loudly. Jennifer, Eric's older sister, had flown in from college. She sat with her arm around her mother, trying to comfort the poor woman.

I stared at them for a while, but I had to look away.

Tears welled in my eyes. I wiped them away with an already wet tissue.

Eric wasn't a close friend. I had gone out with him for a few months last year. I broke up with him when I went back to Bill. Eric didn't seem to care much.

When Honey Perkins showed up last year, she went out with Eric for a short while. She dumped him too. Because she was copying me. Copying everything about me, copying everything I did.

The organ started to play a hymn. I shivered. Not from the cold this time. Thinking about Honey was making me feel even colder.

I glanced at my friends. Trish had her eyes down, hands folded tightly in her lap. Lilah tapped the fingers of both hands nervously against her knees. Her long legs barely fit in the narrow church pew.

My teeth were chattering by the time the service ended. I was desperate to get out of there and warm up. "I'm so cold," I moaned to Trish beside me.

Lilah stood up and stretched. I climbed shakily to my feet. I saw lots of kids and teachers from school. They all looked shaken, dazed by the tragedy.

"Murdered," Trish muttered, shaking her head. Her curly, auburn hair shook with her. "Becka, I can't believe someone we know was murdered."

"Murdered by Honey," I added, my voice a choked whisper. I dabbed at my eyes again. Then I turned to Trish and Lilah. "It was so *frightening* to see Honey again," I said.

"I thought she was far away," Lilah replied. "In a hospital or something. Getting treatment."

"The police said Honey ran away from the hospital last summer," I reported. I'd been so upset since Eric's murder, I hadn't been able to talk to anyone. But now the words poured out of me.

"She never even called her father. He says he had no idea where she was living. I can't believe she's been living in the very next town!" I cried. "And calling herself Becka. Calling herself by *my* name, Becka Norwood."

"Is she in school or anything?" Trish asked. Her normally bright blue eyes were red-rimmed and bloodshot.

"The police said she enrolled at Waynesbridge High—as me!" I replied. I shuddered. "She forged transcripts and everything. She even forged a letter from my parents, saying they wanted me to switch schools because of all the awful things that happened last year. It gives me the creeps just thinking about it."

"It's sick. It's so sick," Lilah murmured, shaking her head.

I could hear Eric's parents sobbing at the front of the church. The coffin stood open. Inside it, I could see Eric's head lying on a dark pillow.

"The police don't know where Honey is living or anything," I told Trish and Lilah. We started walking to the aisle. I nodded to some other kids from school. They nodded solemnly back.

Everyone looked so awful. So sad and dazed and frightened. I could see that some of them had been crying.

I suddenly felt like crying again too. But I took a deep breath and forced back the tears.

"Did she have any friends at Waynesbridge?" Lilah asked. "Any friends who might know where she lives?"

I followed them into the aisle. We walked slowly toward the exit at the back of the church. The organ music droned on.

"The police interviewed a couple of Waynesbridge kids who said they knew her," I replied. "But they had never been to her house. They didn't know where she lived."

"And they thought her name was Becka?" Lilah asked.

I nodded. "Yes. They thought—"

I stopped in midsentence. And gasped.

"Oh no. Noooo," I moaned.

I pointed to the exit. "There she is. There's Honey!"

chapter

12

Trish and Lilah spun around and stared at Honey. I saw Trish shudder. Lilah grabbed my hand as Honey approached us.

"Don't let her near me," I whispered.

Honey had her coppery hair pulled back behind the shoulders of her tan trenchcoat. She walked toward us quickly, her hands shoved into the coat pockets.

"Keep her away—please!" I begged.

"It isn't Honey," Trish murmured.

I turned and realized that both of my friends were staring hard at me. "It isn't her," Trish repeated.

The girl strode past us, heading down the aisle to Eric's family at the front of the church.

I realized I'd been holding my breath. I let it out in a long whoosh. My heart raced.

"We're kind of worried about you, Becka," Lilah said softly. She let go of my hand.

Trish nodded.

"Worried?" I murmured, my eyes still on the girl in the trenchcoat.

"We'll walk you home," Trish offered.

"Thanks," I replied. I took another deep breath, waiting for my heart to slow.

"This isn't the first time you thought you saw Honey," Lilah said, biting her bottom lip.

"I keep seeing her everywhere," I confessed. I hadn't planned to reveal that to them. I didn't want them to think I was crazy or something.

We made our way down the front steps of the church and began to walk slowly down Park Drive. The clouds pulled away from the sun as we passed Shadyside High, and rays of yellow sunlight slanted over the grass.

"We've been kind of worried about you ever since . . . ever since Bill was stabbed," Lilah continued.

I raised a hand to shield my eyes from the bright sunlight. Lilah had to duck her head to walk under a low tree limb that stretched over the sidewalk. Lilah is the tallest girl at Shadyside High. She's tall and slim like a fashion model. I'm so envious of her. But she *hates* being so much taller than us.

"I hope you'll take it in the right way," Trish added, her blue eyes locked on mine. "But you just haven't been the same, Becka."

Lilah stopped walking and turned to me. "Are you okay?" she asked. "I mean, *really* okay?"

"Well . . ." I watched a Shadyside bus rumble past. It moved by, revealing a lanky, blond-haired boy standing on the corner across the street.

I gasped in surprise. "Bill?"

He came trotting across the street. "Hey—hi," he called. He was huffing and puffing by the time he reached us.

I swallowed hard.

Trish gave Bill a peck on the cheek. "How are you?" she asked.

He shrugged, still breathing hard. "Sorry. Let me catch my breath." He motioned to his chest. "I'll never make the track team. But I do pretty well for only one lung!"

I shuddered. I saw the knife again. And the blood all over Honey's kitchen.

I saw the knife every time I was with Bill now. And I pictured the blade penetrating his chest, wrecking one lung.

Bill had been such a good sport about it. So strong. So positive.

"I'm lucky to be alive," he told me. "Every-one thought I was dead. But here I am. One lung should get me through life okay. I'll just take my time."

If only I could be as strong as Bill.

If only I could see him without thinking of that horrible day last winter in Honey's kitchen.

If only I didn't picture all the blood, picture Bill's twisted body sprawled in all that blood on the kitchen floor.

I used to care for Bill so deeply. I went against

my parents' wishes to see him. I sneaked out of the house. I lied about where I was going and who I was seeing.

But now . . . it was different. I had a sick, cold feeling every time I saw him.

I couldn't shake the horrible memory.

I couldn't erase the picture of that knife and all the blood.

I knew it wasn't my fault. But I felt so guilty. I couldn't look Bill in the eye.

I turned to find him staring hard at me. "I heard about Eric," he said softly. He shook his head and scowled. "Honey strikes again."

"It's so awful," Lilah murmured. "So *sick.*"

"Have they caught her?" Bill asked. "Have the police found her?"

"Not yet," I whispered, my throat dry and tight. I stared down at the ground.

"And you saw it, Becka?" Bill asked, his voice rising. "You saw the whole thing?"

I nodded. "Honey tried to make it look as if . . . as if I was the murderer. Just like—" I stopped myself.

Bill grabbed my arm. "Becka, you and I have to talk."

"No," I replied sharply. I backed out of his grasp. "No more talking, Bill."

"Becka, give me a break," he pleaded. "I just want to talk with you. That's all."

I glimpsed Trish and Lilah staring at me, their faces puzzled, concerned.

"I'm all talked out," I told Bill. "I don't want to see you anymore. I can't."

I saw the hurt on his face.

"Becka, I know you're seeing Larry now," Bill continued a little breathlessly. "I know things aren't the way they were. But I just need to get a few things straight between us. I just need to—"

"No. Sorry," I insisted. "Really."

He stared at me for the longest time with those sad, pleading eyes. Then he muttered good-bye to the three of us and walked away, moving slowly, his head down.

I turned away and crossed the street, heading toward home. Trish and Lilah hurried to catch up with me.

"What exactly happened between you two?" Lilah demanded. "You never confided in us, Becka. And we're your best friends."

"Is it because your parents hate Bill so much?" Trish chimed in.

I shook my head. "They've gotten over that," I said flatly. "After . . . after what happened, they actually started to like Bill a little. But . . ." My voice trailed off. I really didn't want to talk about it, even with my best friends.

"But what?" Trish insisted.

Now that the subject had finally been opened, they weren't going to let me off the hook.

"It's just too many bad memories!" I replied heatedly.

"Bill is totally crushed," Trish murmured.

I rolled my eyes. "Tell me something I don't know."

I saw them both staring at me. "I can't help it!" I screamed. "He's a nice guy. Really. But I just can't see him anymore!"

We walked a few blocks in silence. I think they both felt bad about getting me upset. They treated me like some kind of fragile flower. Sometimes I appreciated it. Sometimes it really annoyed me.

The only sound was the creak of the trees in the wind and the crunch of dry, dead leaves under our shoes.

Finally, Trish broke the silence. "Bill was so nice to me when I was in the hospital after my fall," she said, keeping her eyes straight ahead. "I was in such bad shape. I couldn't always see him. But after he recovered, he came to the hospital every day."

I swallowed hard. My mouth felt so dry. A wave of guilt swept over me.

"I wanted to come too, Trish," I told her. "I really did. But . . . it took me so long to get myself together."

"I understand," she replied. But she didn't look at me.

Lilah cleared her throat but didn't say anything.

"It took me so long to stop blaming myself," I continued, my voice trembling. "I blamed myself for what happened to you, Trish. And for Lilah's accident. And for Bill. So much guilt . . ." I took a deep breath. "I'm afraid I wasn't a very good friend to you when you were recovering from that fall, Trish. I . . . I hope I can make it up to you."

She stepped in front of me and threw her arms around me. We hugged for a long time. And then

Lilah hugged me. And all three of us were standing there in the middle of the street, hugging and sobbing.

We're not usually that emotional. I think Eric's funeral put us all on edge.

I felt glad I was finally able to say some of the things I'd been holding inside all these months. But I was also happy to get home a few minutes later, and be by myself, and have some peace and quiet.

I pulled off my coat and started toward the stairs to go up to my room when Mom intercepted me.

"Becka—you're back," she said, eyeing me from head to foot.

I nodded. "It . . . was really sad," I told her. "His family is really messed up."

Mom tsk-tsked. "Are you okay?"

I shrugged. "I guess."

She took my coat from me. Then she tenderly slid the back of her hand down my burning cheek. She's been doing that since I was tiny.

"You sure you're okay? You know Dr. Perlberg said you have to stay calm. You can't let yourself get worked up."

"I had no choice, Mom," I replied sharply. "I had to go to Eric's funeral." I started up the stairs. "I'll be okay," I told her.

I stepped into my room and closed the door behind me.

Peace and quiet at last, I thought.

And the phone rang.

I picked it up and raised it to my ear. "Hello?"

I heard someone breathing.
"Hello? Hello?" I repeated.
Just breathing. Loud, heavy breathing.
Pressing the phone to my ear, I shivered.
Is it Honey? I wondered.
Is she after me now?
Is this just the start?

chapter

13

 Dr. Perlberg thought it would be a good idea for me to get an after-school job. He said it would give me a chance to meet new people and give me new things to think about and occupy my mind.

So I work as a waitress three evenings a week and every other Saturday at a place on Canyon Drive called The Hackers Cafe.

It's actually just a coffeehouse. But Mr. Arnold, the owner, put computers at the counter so that customers could surf the internet and send e-mail while they drink their coffee and eat their muffins and pastries.

The cafe became really popular, especially with kids from Shadyside High and young adults who work in the neighborhood. So the waitress job keeps me pretty busy.

Too busy to stop and chat with my friends.

So the next afternoon, I wasn't exactly happy to see my new boyfriend Larry Myers drop down at the counter and wave to me.

I sighed, walked over to him, and pretended to wipe the counter. "Hi, Larry. What's up?"

He shrugged and gave me his goofy smile. He has a pile of red hair on his head and freckles on his pudgy, little nose. And his two front teeth stick out. Some of the guys call him Bugs Bunny. But I think he's cute.

"Just came to say hi," he said.

"Hi," I replied. "Bye."

He forced an exaggerated hurt expression to his face. Pouting made him look even more comical. "Want me to wait around and drive you home, Becka?"

I moved the napkin holder and pretended to wipe underneath it. "No. I drove."

He pouted some more. "Well . . . could I come over to your house when you get home after work?"

"Not tonight," I told him. "I have so much homework. Ms. Mosely gave us two acts of *King Lear* to read in one night."

"I could rent the movie," Larry suggested. "You wouldn't have to read it."

"I *want* to read it!" I insisted. I glanced over my shoulder. Mr. Arnold was eyeing me from the kitchen. I took out my pad. "Order something," I told Larry.

"Huh?" He narrowed his eyes at me. "You know I don't like coffee. It's too bitter."

"Well, order a doughnut or a muffin or something," I instructed him. I could *feel* the owner's eyes on the back of my neck.

"I don't have any money," Larry confessed.

I laughed. "Bye," I said, turning away.

"No. Let's just talk for a few minutes," he insisted.

I shook my head. "No way. If I lose my job, we'll both be broke. Bye. See you."

He gave me a little wave and started to the door, walking that funny, bobbing walk of his. His expression was pretty forlorn. I realized I hadn't been very nice to him.

"I'll call you when I get home," I shouted.

That appeared to cheer him up. He walked out the door smiling.

Later, I was thinking about Larry as I changed back into my jeans and pullover and tossed my blue-and-white waitress uniform in the laundry hamper.

I was so unfriendly to Larry, so nervous about my job, I scolded myself. Maybe I'll stop by Larry's house just for a few minutes. After all, I need a little break. I can't go right from work to *King Lear*.

I said good night to Mr. Arnold. He gave me the usual two-fingered salute off the front of his bald head. He was the quietest person I ever knew. He communicated with smiles and frowns and little salutes. The only time he ever spoke to any of us workers was when we did something wrong.

I pushed open the cafe door and stepped out onto the parking lot. It was only seven-thirty, but the sky was already dark. The days become so much shorter in the fall. I am always surprised not to find daylight when I come out from work.

I buttoned my jacket. The wind carried a chill. I pulled my hair up with both hands from inside the jacket collar. Then I turned and headed around to the employees' parking lot in back.

The long, narrow lot stood pitch black. Mr. Arnold had forgotten to turn on the lights back here.

I waited for my eyes to adjust, then started walking briskly toward my little Civic at the back of the lot.

I was about halfway to the car when I heard the rapid *thud* of footsteps coming up fast behind me.

I spun around, squinting into the darkness—and gasped.

Honey!

chapter

14

No. Not Honey.

I heard sharp, shallow breathing before the figure stepped into view.

Then I recognized Bill's blond hair, his dark, unhappy eyes, his tense frown.

"Bill—what are you doing here?" I demanded. "You scared me."

"Sorry." He stopped a few feet from me, breathing hard, his chest heaving up and down beneath his leather jacket.

His chest . . . The knife in his chest . . . The blood . . . The knife in my hand . . .

"Bill, I told you yesterday—" I started.

He raised a hand to cut me off. "I just want to talk to you for five minutes, Becka." His voice was shrill, angry.

"Please," I murmured. I glanced at the dark

69

shape of my car. I just wanted to climb inside and drive away. I didn't want a big shouting scene with him here in this empty parking lot.

"I tried to call you yesterday afternoon," he said, lowering his gaze to the ground. "But when I heard your voice, I—I lost my nerve."

"Huh?" My mouth dropped open. "I heard a lot of breathing," I said. "That was *you?*"

He nodded, embarrassed.

I slapped my forehead. "I blamed Honey," I blurted out.

Am I losing my mind? I asked myself. *Am I going to keep seeing Honey everywhere? Keep imagining that she's calling me?*

Bill stepped closer. Even in the darkness, I could see the unhappiness in his eyes, the desperation on his face.

"I still care about you," he said, his voice just above a whisper, so low I could barely hear it over the wind swirling through the parking lot.

"What?" I murmured. "Bill, I—"

"I still care about you, Becka," he repeated, more forcefully. "I can't believe you won't even agree to talk to me. I can't believe you won't see me anymore. I . . . I . . ."

He grabbed my wrist and tried to pull me to him.

"Bill—let go!" I cried.

He tightened his grip. "You have to give me a chance, Becka," he said heatedly. His chest started heaving up and down again.

One lung . . . I thought. *One lung . . .*

"Let go of my arm!" I cried. "You're . . . frightening me!"

"No!" he screamed shrilly. "I won't let go. Not until you promise—"

I jerked back. Struggled to free myself.

But he held on tight.

"Bill—please—!"

I heard footsteps. Shoes scraping on the parking lot asphalt. Running footsteps.

"Larry!" I cried.

Larry came running up to us. He glared furiously at Bill. "I heard Becka say 'let go.'"

Bill stared at his hand gripping my wrist, stared at it as if he didn't recognize it. He let out his breath and released my arm.

He took a step back. His eyes narrowed in confusion. "Sorry," he murmured. "Really. I didn't mean . . ."

Larry turned to me. "Are you okay? Did he hurt you, Becka?"

"No!" Bill cried before I could answer Larry. "No way! I didn't!"

Larry kept his eyes on me. "Are you okay?" he repeated softly.

I rubbed my wrist. "I'm okay," I said. "He just frightened me, that's all."

Bill eyed us both, breathing hard. He took another step back. "I didn't mean anything," he choked out. "I didn't mean to hurt you. I only wanted to talk."

Then he turned and hurried back toward the restaurant and the street.

Larry slid his arm around my shoulder. "What's his problem?" he asked softly.

"You know," I replied. "You know his problem."

He kept his arm around me and guided me to the car.

"What are you doing here?" I asked, still feeling shaky. "I told you I couldn't—"

"I thought maybe you'd change your mind," he said.

We stopped in front of my Civic. I fumbled in my bag for the key. I found it and stuck it into the door.

"That's weird," I murmured. "The door isn't locked. You know I always lock it."

"Maybe you forgot this time," Larry suggested.

I shrugged.

And pulled open the door.

The roof light came on.

And I let out a scream of horror.

chapter

15

"This isn't my car!" I shrieked. "This isn't my car!"

I heard the words escape my mouth—but I felt as if someone else was screaming them.

As if someone else was staring in at the disgusting, frightening scene.

As if I was standing outside myself, watching myself press my hands to the sides of my face and scream and scream and scream.

Larry had his arm around me. He tried to talk to me, to calm me down, to comfort me.

But I had flipped out of control, and there was nothing he could do about it. Nothing I could do about it.

"It isn't my car! It *can't* be my car!"

I gaped in openmouthed horror at the slashed seats. Cut to pieces. Chunks of foam rubber ripped out and strewn across the torn strips of fabric.

And what was that on the passenger seat?

What *was* that?

Ohhhhh . . .

A rat. A fat gray rat. Dead . . .

Its stomach . . . its whole front . . . ripped open. Slashed open and its guts pouring out on my seat . . . on my car seat . . . cut open like a piece of ripe fruit . . . dripping . . . pouring . . .

Little black eyes staring up at the car light.

Stomach open, red . . . and glistening wet.

Ohhhh . . .

"Honey did this! It had to be Honey!"

Was that *me* shrieking her name at the top of my lungs?

"Honey! Honey! Honey!"

I saw the startled, frightened look on Larry's face. But there wasn't anything I could do about it.

No way I could stop shrieking.

"Honey! Honey! Honey!"

I don't remember Larry leading me to his car. And I don't remember him helping me inside it.

When I stopped screaming, we were nearly at my house on Fear Street.

Larry stared straight ahead through the windshield, his features set hard, jaw clenched, eyes unblinking, arms rigid as he gripped the top of the wheel.

He didn't look at all like Bugs Bunny.

Mom gave me two of the pills Dr. Perlberg had prescribed as a sedative. After a short while, I began to feel calmer.

I felt so awful. I had gone for so many months without losing it like that.

I hadn't needed Dr. Perlberg's pills since last spring.

But, of course, that's because Honey was away. Honey was out of my life.

I wanted to call Larry and apologize. But I was afraid of what he would say.

Does he think I'm totally messed up now? I wondered.

Will he be afraid to be with me? Afraid I'll freak out like that again?

Up in my bedroom, I took a hot shower and changed into my comfy flannel nightshirt. Then I turned on the TV to distract me.

What a mistake.

I turned it on just in time to see a news story about Honey.

". . . Police are still investigating the murder of a teenager at the Division Street Mall . . ." I heard a deep-voiced reporter say.

The picture flashed on. A black-and-white photo of Eric from last year's yearbook filled the screen.

"The alleged strangler of Eric Fraser, a high school student named Honey Perkins, is still at large . . ."

Eric's photo was replaced by a view of The Clothes Hangar, the store where poor Eric was killed. Shoppers were shaking their heads and staring down at a black body outline on the floor of the store.

"The police," the reporter continued, "have a statewide hunt on for the alleged murderer."

I flicked off the TV and tossed the remote across the room.

"A statewide hunt?" I screeched. "She's right here in Shadyside!"

I dropped onto my bed. Jumped up. Paced the room. Dropped back onto the bed again.

I didn't know where to put myself. I didn't know what to do.

The pills weren't helping at all.

The news report had made me crazy all over again.

Honey was right here in Shadyside. I was certain of it.

She wrecked my car tonight. She slashed the seats and murdered a rat and spread its guts all over my car.

They don't need a statewide hunt. She's right here. Right here. Right here.

I pulled open my window.

So hot . . . so stifling hot.

I needed to breathe some fresh air. I needed to feel some cool air on my face.

I took a deep breath. Then another.

I stared down at the house next door.

And uttered a low cry.

The house next door. Honey's father's house.

Honey had moved next door to me last fall. That's when all my trouble started. When Honey and her father moved next door.

That's where Bill was stabbed. In Honey's kitchen next door.

Next door . . .

As I stared down at the house, the moon slid behind clouds. The house appeared to back into deep shadows.

76

I knew that Honey's father still lived there. Alone.

But was he alone in there now?

Had Honey returned? Was she hiding in there?

A cold shiver rolled down my back. My entire body trembled.

Was Honey right next door?

I had to find out. I had to know.

I turned away from my window. My hands trembled as I pulled on my clothes.

I took a deep breath and held it, trying to calm myself. Then I headed out to get my coat.

chapter

16

My phone rang as I reached the bed-room door.

I stopped in the doorway, turned, and stared at the phone.

Should I answer it? Or should I go check out the house next door?

I let it ring twice. Three times.

Then I dove across the room and lifted it to my ear. "Hello?"

"Hi, Becka. It's me."

"Hi, Trish. What's up?" I replied impatiently. I held the phone between my shoulder and cheek, and buttoned the cuffs on my shirt.

"Can we talk? Do you have a few minutes?" Trish sounded troubled.

"Yeah. Sure." I dropped onto the edge of the bed, still struggling with a button. "Are you okay, Trish?" I asked. "You sound . . . weird."

78

"I'm okay," she assured me. "It's Bill."

"Excuse me?" I cried. "What about Bill?" The phone slipped from my shoulder. I grabbed it in my hand and returned it to my ear.

"Bill was just here, Becka," Trish reported. "He came over after dinner to talk to me. He . . . he's totally messed up."

I sighed and wearily ran my free hand back through my hair. It felt greasy. I was really in need of a shampoo.

"Bill is messed up? You mean, about *me?*" I demanded.

"Yeah," Trish replied. "About you. He wants another chance, Becka. He thinks you're being really unfair to him."

"That's what he told you?" I asked shrilly. "He came over to your house—to my best friend's house—to complain about how I won't talk to him?"

Silence at Trish's end for a long moment. Then she said softly, "He's very hurt, Becka. Do you know what he did? He pulled up his shirt and showed me the scar where Honey stabbed him."

"He *what?*" I cried. I jumped to my feet and began pacing back and forth, pressing the phone to my ear. "He showed you his scar?"

"Bill said that you hurt him even more than that knife," Trish repeated, lowering her voice nearly to a whisper.

I uttered a sharp cry.

"That isn't fair," I said. I had a tight feeling in my throat, as if I had something caught in it. "That really isn't fair at all."

I began pacing faster. My temples throbbed. I coughed, trying to clear my dry throat.

"I'm just telling you what he said," Trish insisted. "He's so messed up, Becka. You should have seen him."

"Hmmmmmm." I knew I was supposed to feel guilty. But at that moment, I felt only anger. "Whose side are you on, Trish?" I cried into the phone.

My question must have startled her. I heard her gasp. But she didn't reply.

"Whose side are you on?" I repeated. "You know why I can't see Bill. You know how upset I get when I see him. He makes me remember too much, Trish. He brings back that whole frightening time of my life."

I nearly dropped the phone again. I held it with both hands and pressed it to my ear. "I have to forget about last year," I continued, unable to keep the emotion from my voice. "You know I have to get over it and move on with my life. The doctor says I have to forget about it. I *want* to forget about it—do you understand?"

"I know, Becka, but—"

"I can't believe you would call me and stick up for Bill," I told Trish angrily.

"I'm not sticking up for him," she insisted. "I just think you're being unfair. I mean—"

"Unfair?" I shrieked, losing control. *"Unfair?* Don't you have any idea what I've been through?"

I was too angry to keep talking to her. I clicked the phone off and tossed it onto the bed.

I crossed my arms tightly in front of me to stop

myself from shaking. And I continued to pace furiously back and forth the length of my room.

She's a traitor! I told myself.

She's no friend.

The phone rang.

I stopped and stared at it. I knew it was Trish calling to apologize. I let it ring a couple of times. Then I picked it up.

I couldn't stay angry at her. We'd been friends for too long. And she wasn't trying to hurt me, I knew. She was only trying to help.

"I'm sorry, Trish," I started.

But the voice at the other end wasn't Trish's.

"You killed Bill!" I heard in a harsh, raspy whisper.

Huh? I thought. Bill isn't dead.

"Who is this?" I cried. "Honey? Is that you?"

"You killed Bill," the voice rasped. *"You killed Bill."*

chapter

17

A few minutes later, I sneaked downstairs and silently pulled my coat from the front closet. I could hear murmured voices from inside my parents' room. They were still awake, but I didn't care.

I had to sneak next door. I had to know if Honey was there, making her sick phone calls from her father's house.

She's trying to drive me crazy, I realized.

Somehow, I've got to stop her, I decided. I'm already a wreck, a nervous wreck.

She's a murderer.

She strangled poor Eric in front of an entire store.

Is she going to try to kill me next? Is that her plan?

Is she going to torture me with phone calls first? Frighten me until I'm a weak, trembling mess?

Then murder me so that she can be Becka from now on?

I can't let her. I can't.

These were my thoughts as I crept out the front door. The cold, crisp air felt good against my hot cheeks. I carefully closed the door behind me. And gazed at the Perkinses' house next door.

A low hedge separated our front yards. The hedge hadn't been trimmed in a while. Fat, dead leaves were tangled in it.

Clouds covered the moon. The house rose up darkly, black against the charcoal sky. A metal gutter along the side of the house creaked in the wind.

I stepped off my front stoop. My sneakers slipped on the dew-slick grass.

Next door, the front of the house lay in total darkness. But as I approached, I saw that a window near the back glowed with a pale orange light.

I stopped and stared at the rectangle of light. Someone is home, I realized.

Is it Honey? Is she in there?

Another thought sent a chill down my back: Is Honey at one of the dark windows, watching me as I approach?

Waiting for me?

That thought almost forced me to turn back. I had a strong urge to run back to the safety of my house.

But I realized that my house wasn't safe at all. Not while Honey was around. I had to know if she was in there. I couldn't be safe—I couldn't sleep— if she were there.

Keeping my eyes on the lighted window, I crept

through an opening in the hedge. My arm brushed the shrub as I passed, making a big section of the hedge tremble.

The light was in a bedroom, I decided. I knew the kitchen stood on the other side of the house. Was it Mr. Perkins's room?

Or was it Honey's?

I swallowed hard and made my way slowly, silently, across the yard.

The light washed out of the window, down the shingled wall of the house, spilling onto the tall grass. I peered into the window from a distance. But it was smeared and covered with droplets of water.

I couldn't see anything.

Closer, I urged myself. You have to go closer, Becka.

My heart pounding, my hands suddenly ice cold, I crept closer, moving slowly, a step at a time.

I was only a few feet from the side of the house when my foot landed on top of something lying in the grass.

Something solid—but soft.

A body?

"**O**hhhhh."

A low moan escaped my throat. I jerked my foot away.

I lowered my eyes—and stared down at a large burlap bag. A bag of lawn fertilizer.

Not a body. Not a body.

Trembling all over, I struggled to catch my breath.

Honey is doing this to me, I told myself. Honey is making me imagine horrible things. She has frightened me so much I can't think straight.

I'm seeing dead bodies everywhere I go.

I took a deep breath and held it. I waited for my temples to stop throbbing.

A shadow moved across the lighted bedroom window. Was someone inside approaching the window?

I dove to the house and pressed myself flat

against the shingled wall. Then slowly, slowly, I edged up to the window.

Carefully, I moved in front of the window, gazing into the yellow light. I half expected to see Honey staring out at me.

But no. No one there.

My heart thudding, I pressed my face close to the smeared pane and peered inside.

I saw the flickering light of a TV screen.

And then, as my eyes slowly adjusted, I saw a man slouched in a tattered, brown armchair in front of the TV. Mr. Perkins. Dressed in a flannel shirt and baggy gray sweatpants. Holding a can of beer in his lap with one hand.

His head was tilted down. Beneath his flannel shirt, his chest rose and fell over his big belly.

He's asleep, I realized. He fell asleep in front of the TV.

The beer can tipped in his hand but didn't fall. His mouth opened and closed with each breath.

His other hand moved. It brushed the arm of the chair, the stubby fingers opening and closing.

Honey's dad. He seems to be all alone.

I squinted through the glass at him, unable to take my eyes away.

I haven't seen him since Honey went to the hospital, I suddenly realized.

In all this time, I never saw him.

Does he ever come out of the house? Doesn't he go to work in the morning and come home at night?

How is it possible that in almost a year—an entire year—I've never seen him?

Leaning against the stone window ledge, I stared

in at him for a few seconds more. Then I let my eyes wander around the small room, searching for a sign, any sign that Honey was in there too.

Nothing more to see here, I decided. He seems to be alone. But I can't really be sure. Maybe I'll head around to the back and see if any other lights are on.

I let go of the window ledge. Took a step back.

And two hands grabbed me roughly from behind.

chapter

19

"No—!"

I uttered a scream—and struggled free.

"Honey—!" I cried.

Off balance, I spun around—and stared at Lilah's startled face.

"Huh?"

I let out a gasp and grabbed on to her to keep myself from falling.

"Becka—I'm sorry!" Lilah whispered. "I didn't mean to scare you. I thought—"

"You scared me to death!" I cried. Then I clapped a hand over my mouth.

I'd cried out too loudly.

I whirled around to the lighted window, expecting to see Honey's father staring out at us.

No. Not there.

"Lilah—you should never sneak up behind me

like that," I scolded her, still breathing hard. "I thought it was Honey. I thought she caught me back here and—"

"I'm so sorry, Becka." She grabbed my ice-cold hand and held on to it. "I didn't mean to scare you. I thought you saw me coming. I really did."

She gazed up at the window. "What are you doing over here, Becka?" she demanded. "It's so late."

"What are *you* doing here?" I shot back. I pulled my hand free and shoved my hands into my coat pockets. I shivered.

"I came over to show you something," she replied, tossing back her hair. "I parked on the street in front of your house. I didn't know if you were still awake. Then I saw you creeping around over here."

Lilah raised her eyes to the window. "What are you doing, Becka? Are you spying on Honey's dad?"

I opened my mouth to answer.

But before I could get a sound out, the window slid open.

Lilah and I both cried out and spun around.

Mr. Perkins leaned forward, stuck his bald head out the open window, and glared at us. "Who's there?" he called out, his voice still gruff from sleep.

Lilah staggered back, her eyes wide with fright.

"I—we—uh—" I sputtered.

Mr. Perkins squinted harder at me. After a few seconds, he seemed to recognize me.

"You?" he cried hoarsely. He started to clear his throat, but it turned into a long, wet coughing fit.

"Get away from here!" he cried when he finally finished coughing. He shook a finger angrily at me. "Haven't you caused enough trouble?"

"Sorry," I murmured. "I didn't mean . . ." I took a step back. I had the urge to turn and run. I glanced at Lilah. She was staring at me, waiting to see how I handled this.

"Where is Honey?" Mr. Perkins demanded suddenly, bellowing at the top of his lungs. "Where is she?"

"I—I don't know," I stammered.

"Where is she?" he repeated. I could smell the beer on his breath. "Do you know where she is? Do you?"

"No!" I cried. "I don't know." I glanced again at Lilah. She motioned to my house with her eyes.

"I have to go home now," I told Mr. Perkins.

"Where is Honey?" he rasped. "Where is she?"

"I really don't know," I repeated.

"If I catch you here again, I'll call the cops!" he threatened. He leaned farther out the window. "Think I'm kidding? Try me. I'll call the cops."

"I'm really sorry—" I started.

But he slammed the window shut before I could finish.

I turned back to Lilah with a shudder. "Whew!"

"Nice guy," she muttered.

I started to laugh. It was the way Lilah said it. Or maybe it was just relief that he had shut the window and gone back inside.

"Let's nominate him for a Good Neighbor Award," Lilah joked, shaking her head.

And now we were both laughing. It wasn't really funny, but we were laughing anyway.

And then we were running side by side across the lawn, through the low hedge, and to my house.

I raised a finger to my lips as we entered. "I don't know if my parents are asleep or not," I told Lilah. "But I don't want them to hear us."

We crept up the stairs to my room, and I closed the door behind us. We both tossed our coats to the floor and dropped down on the edge of the bed.

I sighed. "That man is such a creep," I said. "He really frightened me."

"Me too," Lilah confessed. "And I have shocking news for you, Becka."

"Huh? What news?" I demanded.

She lowered her voice to a whisper. "He isn't Honey's father," she said.

"What do you mean?" I demanded.

"This is what I came to show you," Lilah replied. She climbed off the bed and picked her coat up off the floor. Then she searched her coat pockets until she found what she was looking for.

She held it up and let her coat fall back down. "Check this out, Becka."

I took it from her hand. A wrinkled, yellowed newspaper clipping.

"My mother found this," Lilah said, dropping down next to me on the bed. "Read it, Becka. You're not going to believe it."

chapter

20

I raised the old newspaper clipping closer and read the bold, black headline: MURDER-SUICIDE BAFFLES SHADYSIDE POLICE.

"How old is this story?" I asked Lilah.

She shoved the clipping back up to my face. "Read. Just read."

I squinted at the faded type and started to read the old news story:

Nine-year-old Hannah Paulsen is the only eyewitness to the tragedy that destroyed her family. But so far, Shadyside police have had little luck in getting the girl to help them put together the pieces of the story.

Hannah remains in shock at Shadyside General Hospital.

Neighbors of the Paulsens are also in shock. Those interviewed say they cannot believe that

93

Mr. Kevin Paulsen murdered his wife Dierdre and Hannah's twin brother Harold, and then shot himself to death. Hannah, hidden in a closet, watched the entire scene through a crack in the door.

"Whoa!" I murmured, lowering the clipping to my lap. "This is a horrible story."

"But don't you remember?" Lilah cried excitedly. "Becka—don't you remember Hannah and Harold?"

And then, as if someone had lifted a curtain from my memory, I *did* remember.

I remembered them both. The Paulsen twins. Hannah and Harold. "They went to our school!" I cried. "They were in our class at Shadyside Elementary!"

"Yes!" Lilah nodded. "Don't you remember? They were both big and kind of nerdy? Total klutzes."

"Oh, wow," I murmured. "Harold and Hannah. They were weird kids." I pressed my hand to my cheek. "I haven't thought about them in years."

I shut my eyes and pictured the Paulsen twins. "I remember them so clearly now, Lilah," I said. "They were both in our class until fourth grade."

"That's when the murders occurred," Lilah said, excitedly pointing to the clipping. "When we were in fourth grade."

I gazed at her. "You mean—"

The story was beginning to sink in. I was finally beginning to realize why Lilah was so excited about finding this old news clipping. Why she couldn't wait to bring it to me.

"Harold's father shot him to death," Lilah said, taking the clipping from my hand, her eyes scanning it as she talked. "Hannah was the only survivor in the family. She was sent to live with an uncle."

"I remember watching something about a murder on TV," I told Lilah, thinking back. "My parents clicked the TV off. They didn't want me to see. In school, kids whispered about it. But our teacher never told us the truth."

"Miss Gully," Lilah recalled, shaking her head. "She was such a wimp. Remember that cellophane thing she used to wear on her head when it rained?"

"She never told us why Hannah and Harold vanished from class," I remembered. "One day, they were just gone."

"Hannah was a total drip—remember?" Lilah said, frowning.

And more memories pushed their way back into my mind. More memories swept over me like a strong ocean wave.

Hannah . . .

No one liked her. She was so big and clumsy. And . . . needy.

I pictured her grabbing all the cookies off the tray in the lunchroom. I pictured her shoving some little first-graders out of the way to get to the water fountain first.

And I remembered her following me around. Following me down the halls in school, following me home after school. Hannah . . . so eager, so desperate to be my best friend.

But I was always popular. I always had a lot of

friends. Trish and Lilah were my best friends then. And a girl named Julie. And two boys, both named Brian.

We hung out together all the time. Hannah tried to be our friend too. But we never wanted Hannah around. She was so big and dumb and so shabbily dressed. And she was grabby and whiny and no fun at all.

I was embarrassed that she wanted to be my friend. I tried to ignore her. When my friends were around, I didn't talk to her at all.

But that didn't work. She still kept following me everywhere, sitting next to me, hanging around in my yard, waiting for me to come out.

Ignoring her didn't get rid of her. So I tried being mean to her.

"Remember that unbelievably cruel trick we played on Hannah?" Lilah asked.

I stared at her. "Lilah—you're reading my mind. I was just thinking about that."

"It was the beginning of the school year," Lilah recalled. "The beginning of fourth grade. We were all so sick and tired of Hannah hanging around, pestering us."

"I remember," I said quietly.

And I did remember. And I felt embarrassed about what we did . . .

We invited Hannah over to my house after school one day. Trish and Lilah were there. All of us. All the "cool" kids I hung out with.

Hannah was so pleased and thrilled that we actually invited her over. I remember her red cheeks, her wide, excited eyes.

We told her that we had a special club. A "cool" club. And we told her that we wanted her to join.

Hannah went ballistic, I remember. She jumped up and down and clapped her hands. She did a wild cartwheel right in my living room. She was such a klutz. She nearly kicked a vase off the coffee table!

We told her if she wanted to join, she had to do one thing first. For the initiation.

We told her she had to climb onstage during the school assembly the next day. And she had to get down on all fours and bark like a dog.

"Is that all?" Hannah asked. "Is that all I have to do?"

My friends and I wanted to explode with laughter. I don't know how we held it in.

"Yes," I told Hannah. "That's all you have to do to be a member of the Cool Club—for life!"

Well, the next day at assembly in the auditorium, we were all waiting to see if she would do it. And of course she did.

Hannah climbed up on the stage while the principal was speaking. She dropped to all fours, tilted her head up, and howled like a hound dog.

Did we laugh? The whole school laughed so hard, the auditorium shook.

Hannah turned bright red and crawled off the stage.

That afternoon when she came over to my house, I told her the bad news. That there *was* no Cool Club. That we just made it up as a joke.

"From now on," I told Hannah, "maybe you'll stop following us around like a puppy."

Hannah opened her mouth and began to sob.

Huge teardrops poured down her cheeks. She raised her fists in the air. I thought she was going to slug me.

But no. She turned and ran off, sobbing at the top of her lungs.

I never saw her again.

And I never knew why.

I guess her family was murdered soon after that.

And now I felt cold all over, cold and ashamed. Ashamed that I'd been so cruel to that poor little girl.

I turned to Lilah. I tried to cough and clear the lump from my throat. But I couldn't get rid of it.

I pressed my hands together tightly in my lap. My stomach suddenly felt as if it had been tied in knots.

"Hannah is Honey," I murmured softly.

Lilah nodded.

"Hannah is Honey," I repeated. "And now I know why Honey hates me so much."

I shuddered.

She just wanted to be my best friend. And I humiliated her. I made her bark like a dog in front of the whole school.

And so she had come back last year. Still determined to be my best friend. She had come back, so sick and twisted. Wanting to be my best friend.

And wanting to destroy me at the same time.

"Oh, wow, Lilah," I moaned. "I'm really scared now."

Lilah nodded solemnly.

"Honey killed Eric," I murmured. "Now she's threatening me. I know she plans to kill me too. I know it."

"You have to stay calm," Lilah warned. "Look at you, Becka. You're shaking all over."

She squeezed my hand. "You've got to find some help. You can't let this ruin your life. It took you so long to get your strength back—after last year."

"I know." I sighed. "Believe me, I know."

"Honey could be a million miles away by now," Lilah continued. "You don't really know that she's after you. Sure, she pretended to be you. But now that she's been found out, she probably took off."

"I don't think so, Lilah," I replied in a whisper. "I know you're trying to comfort me. But . . . I think Honey is nearby. I really do."

"Becka, listen to me—" Lilah started. But she didn't get to finish her sentence.

The phone rang.

We both jumped.

I grabbed it up without thinking. "Hello? Who is it?" I choked out.

"It's me again, Becka," a whispery voice rasped.

"No—!" I gasped.

"It's me," the voice whispered. "Your best friend. I'm coming to see you, Becka. I have something for you. Something shiny and sharp."

part
3

chapter

21

Dr. Perlberg waved me to the couch. "Do you want to lie down and talk, Becka? Or do you want to sit?"

I turned from the couch to the black leather armchair in front of his cluttered desk. "I—I don't know," I stammered. I had been clenching my jaw so tight, my teeth hurt. "Sit, I guess."

Sunlight poured in through the open blinds on the window behind the desk. It hurt my eyes. I hadn't slept all night.

"Then have a seat." He motioned to the chair, his eyes studying me behind his black-framed glasses. He wore a pale blue dress shirt over gray slacks. He had pulled his dark striped tie loose at his neck.

I sank into the straight-backed armchair. I wrapped my hands around the leather arms. Then I clasped and unclasped them tensely in my lap.

Did I remember to brush my hair? I suddenly wondered.

I'd been a total mess all day. It was a miracle I made it out of the house at all.

"You said on the phone that you were troubled," Dr. Perlberg said softly. He lowered his large body into his desk chair and searched through the stacks of papers on the desk until he found a long, yellow writing pad.

"Troubled?" A bitter laugh escaped my throat. "Dr. Perlberg, I can't think straight. I'm so frightened."

He set down his pencil and leaned across the desk, studying me. "Tell me what's happening, Becka," he said softly. "Take your time, okay? Sit back, take a deep breath, then tell me what's going on."

I told him about Honey. At first, I didn't know where to begin. My words came out jumbled. I had spent so many hours over the past year talking with him about Honey, so many days and days.

I didn't want to be sitting in this cramped little office talking about her now. I wanted that ugly part of my life to be over.

But it wasn't over.

And now I knew it wouldn't be over until Honey was caught.

I told him about Honey pretending to be me at Waynesbridge High. I told him how Honey murdered Eric at the mall, how I watched as she strangled him.

Dr. Perlberg had already read about the murder in the newspaper. He already knew all the details. But he made me tell the story anyway.

I told him about creeping out to spy on Honey's father. Except, he isn't her father. He's her uncle.

I told him about the old newspaper clipping. I explained how Honey was actually Hannah. And then I told him about her latest phone call.

"She called and threatened me," I choked out. I clasped my cold hands tighter in my lap. "She said she's coming for me, with a knife. She's going to stab me, the way she stabbed Bill."

Dr. Perlberg let out a sigh. "The police?"

"They can't find her," I replied in a trembling voice. "They haven't caught her."

He shook his head. "No. I meant, did you call the police? Did you tell them about the threat Honey made on the phone?"

I hesitated. "No. I—I was so afraid. I didn't—" I squeezed the chair arms. My hands were dripping wet. They left wet smears on the leather.

"I need more of those pills," I blurted out. "To calm me down."

He nodded. "That's no problem. I can prescribe something," he said. "But the first thing you have to do, Becka, is talk to your parents. Have them call the police immediately about Honey's phone threat. And have them show the police the old newspaper clipping."

"Okay," I agreed. "I know I should have told them, but—"

"No buts," he said firmly. "Just do it—as soon as you get home."

He scribbled something on the pad, then raised his eyes to me. "I want you to check in with me every day, Becka. Don't try to deal with this by yourself," he instructed me. "Make sure you confide in your parents. Make sure you have help all the time. As we know, Honey is truly dangerous."

"Yes," I replied in a whisper. "Honey is dangerous."

Five minutes later, I found out—again—how dangerous Honey could be.

chapter

22

I stepped out of Dr. Perlberg's office feeling shaky and upset. I expected to feel better after talking to him. But I realized I would never feel better until Honey was caught.

It was a warm day for fall. Even the breeze felt warm. Our last blast of summery weather.

So why was I shivering? Why did I feel so cold?

I squinted into the bright sunlight. It reflected off the cars in the small parking lot. Shielding my eyes with one hand, I started toward my little Civic, parked against the wall at the back of the lot.

I stopped when I saw a bright glint of silvery light.

A reflection in my rearview mirror.

I narrowed my eyes, studying the car. What caused that flash of light?

I took a few cautious steps toward the car.

And saw another flash of light. And heard a cough.

A girl's cough.

From behind my car?

"Who's there?" I called. My cry came out shrill and weak. "Is someone back there?"

I heard soft laughter. Cold laughter.

And saw another silvery glint. Off a knife blade?

My whole body tensed. My muscles tightened until I froze, rigid as a statue. "Honey?" I called.

Silence.

"Honey? Are you back there?"

Becka, it's just sunlight, I told myself. You're totally paranoid. There is no one back there holding a knife.

I forced my muscles to relax. I took a step.

And then she sprang out from behind the car.

"Honey—!"

Glowing like fire in the bright sunlight, her hair flew wildly about her head. Her eyes were wild with fury. She opened her mouth in a loud screech.

She raised both hands as if preparing to pounce—and ran at me, roaring ferociously.

I stumbled back, startled.

The sunlight glinted off a silver bracelet on one of her wrists.

In my terror, I pictured a hospital bracelet on that wrist.

But Honey wasn't in a hospital now. Honey was on the loose.

"Honey—no!" I screamed. And then I forced myself to turn away from her and run.

Too late.

I moved three or four steps.

I heard her loud grunt as her arms wrapped around my legs.

She tackled me from behind, and we both fell hard to the asphalt.

She landed heavily on top of me.

"Ohhh." I let out a gasp as my breath was knocked out of me.

Dazed, I tried to roll out from under her.

But she had me pinned to the ground. She sprawled on top of me, grunting, panting like a crazed animal.

I screamed in pain as she dug her knees into my back.

And then I felt her fists furiously pounding my shoulders.

"Honey—stop! Honey!" I shrieked.

She pulled my hair. Tugged it hard with both hands.

"No! Get off!" I wailed. "Get off!"

I kicked and thrashed my arms helplessly.

I couldn't get her off.

Her knees dug into my back.

And then I felt her hands wrap around my head. Her fingers dug into my cheeks.

She began to twist my head. Twist it. Twist it . . .

"Let go of me!" I begged. "Honey—let go . . ."

chapter

23

*H*oney uttered a low grunt and pushed my face into the asphalt.

Then she pulled my head up by the hair.

"Please—" I begged.

I couldn't squirm free. I couldn't grab her.

I couldn't move.

She kneeled on top of me, knees digging into my back, hands holding my head down.

Pain shot through my whole body.

"Honey—I know who you are!" I cried. "I know the whole story!"

She was breathing so loudly, I wasn't sure she heard me. But her hands loosened their grip on my hair. She leaned over me. I felt drops of hot saliva on the back of my neck.

"Honey—" I pleaded. "I mean, Hannah. Let me up. Let me up, please!"

She didn't budge.

"Please—let's talk. Please!"

She didn't move.

"I know everything, Hannah," I choked out. "I'll try to be your friend. I'll try to help you. Really, Hannah. Really. I'll be your friend, Hannah. I promise!"

"I'm not Hannah!" she shrieked.

Her hands tightened around my hair again and pulled my head back . . . back . . .

. . . Until I heard my neck crack.

"I'm not Hannah! And I'm not Honey!" Her knees burrowed into my back.

"Please—" I begged.

"I'm Becka now!" she screamed. "You're not Becka! *I'm* Becka! I'm Becka! I'm Becka!"

She slammed my face into the pavement.

"I'm Becka!"

"I'm Becka!"

I groaned in pain. Cinders and small stones dug into my cheeks and forehead.

Gripping my head with both hands, she shoved my face to the asphalt. Again.

Again.

My head throbbed. Blood trickled from my cut cheeks to the pavement.

"Honey . . ." I called her name in a weak whisper.

But she furiously slammed my head down. Slammed me.

I couldn't move. I couldn't breathe.

111

The pain . . . the pain was so intense . . .

The parking lot . . . the sunlight . . . It was all fading, fading away.

I knew I was going to die.

chapter

24

I blinked. Once. Twice.

Bright light invaded my eyes.

I groaned and lifted my head. And squinted around.

I recognized the parking lot. I recognized the back of the brick building where Dr. Perlberg had his office.

I was sprawled facedown on the asphalt, a few yards from my car.

"Alive," I murmured aloud. "I'm alive."

I spit strands of hair from my mouth. Brushing my hand over my face, I felt caked blood on my chin, my cheeks.

"Ohhh." Everything hurt.

I raised myself to a sitting position. Tried to rub the aching pain from the back of my neck. I felt my nose. Was it broken?

No. Just cut.

113

My face must look like raw meat, I thought.

But I'm alive.

Why?

I gazed around the small lot. Where was Honey? Why did she leave?

I pushed a clump of hair off my forehead. It felt sticky, damp. From blood, I realized.

Honey must think that she killed me.

That's what I decided as I slowly climbed to my feet.

She thinks she killed me.

She thinks she's free to be Becka now.

I stood up, fighting off my dizziness.

"Maybe I'll never see her again," I murmured out loud. My mouth felt dry, my tongue swollen.

If Honey thinks I'm dead, maybe she won't come after me again.

No more threats. No more attacks.

No, I decided. That's too much to hope for.

I picked my bag up off the pavement and searched through it. Did Honey leave me my car keys?

Yes.

I pulled them out. My hand trembled so much, the keys slipped from my fingers. They clattered to the ground. I bent and scooped them up, and stumbled to my car.

It felt so good to sit behind the wheel in silence. Alone. The doors locked.

Safe and alone.

I wrapped my trembling hands around the wheel and started to sob. Angry tears, bitter tears, rolled down my burning cheeks.

I was so messed up, so dizzy and hurt and frightened. How did I ever manage to drive home?

I'm not sure. I don't remember driving. I don't remember the ride at all.

But a few minutes later, I pulled the car up the driveway. And ran inside to tell my mom what had happened.

After dinner, I called Trish and told her about Honey and how she attacked me in the parking lot. Trish kept gasping and muttering, "Oh wow. Oh wow."

"She tried to kill me," I told Trish. "I really think she was trying to kill me." I tenderly rubbed my sore cheek.

"Did you tell the police?" Trish demanded.

"Well, first Mom took me to the emergency room," I reported. "I was pretty much okay. But Mom said we had to make sure. Dad met us there, and he was a total basket case. He called the police on his cell phone right from the hospital. He insisted that they come to the hospital, to the emergency room and see what I look like."

"Oh wow," Trish murmured. "Your face, Becka—is it really messed up?"

"It's pretty bruised." I sighed. "Especially my forehead. I needed a few stitches on my forehead. Right over my eyebrow. But the other cuts should heal okay."

I sighed again. "Too bad it isn't Halloween."

"I don't see how you can joke about it," Trish said heatedly.

"What else can I do?" I replied. "I look like

Frankenstein. But I guess I'm lucky to be alive. Anyway, once I changed my clothes and we washed all the blood out of my hair and off my face, I looked a lot better."

"Oh wow. What did the police say?" Trish asked.

"They said they'd put a regular patrol on my block," I told her.

"That's all?" Trish cried.

"I guess they're doing everything they can to catch her," I said. I moved the phone to the other ear because my cheek started to hurt. "The officer said it would be easier to find her, now that they know she's close by."

"I hope so," Trish said softly.

"I hope so too," I replied with a shudder. I stared out the window at Honey's uncle's house next door. "I hope so too," I repeated.

On Sunday night, Larry picked me up in his father's Range Rover, and we drove to the tenplex at the mall. We rode most of the way in silence, staring out at a drizzling rain.

Larry kept trying to make conversation. But I barely said a word. I guess I still felt afraid to go out.

I couldn't stop thinking about Honey. I kept picturing her behind every house, every tree, every car.

I felt bad, because Larry had been terrific for the past few days. He had been so nice to me, so caring.

He came over every day. He called me every night. And he never said that my face looked like a lump of canned dog food, although I'm sure he thought it.

"I'm sorry," I said as we turned off Division Street into the vast mall parking lot.

He braked to let some kids on Rollerblades skate past, and turned to me. "Huh? Sorry?"

"Sorry that I'm in such a bad mood," I said. "Sorry that I'm no fun."

He squeezed my hand. "You don't have to be fun. Who says you have to be fun?"

I laughed. I knew he was being silly, trying to cheer me up.

But how could I cheer up?

"I just have the feeling that Honey is going to come back to finish the job," I confessed.

He circled the area in front of the movie theater, searching for a parking space. "You mean—?"

"I mean, I think she's going to come back and try to kill me," I said, my voice cracking. I cleared my throat. I had a hard knot there, a tension knot, I guess. I kept clearing my throat all day, but I couldn't get rid of it.

"You think she's following you?" Larry asked.

I shrugged. "No. Yes. I don't know. She followed me to Dr. Perlberg's office, didn't she? She could be following me right now."

Larry peered into the rearview mirror. "I don't see anyone."

"She could be here at the mall already," I insisted. "Waiting for me. Waiting to kill me."

Larry curled his lips in a low whistle. He pulled the big Range Rover into a narrow space near the back of the lot. He cut the lights and switched off the ignition.

Then he turned to me. "Did Honey call you again?" he asked.

"Yes." I bit my bottom lip. "She's called every night. She whispers to disguise herself. I don't know why. I know it's her."

"Every night?" Larry shook his head.

"Yes," I replied. "And she says the most horrible things. She says she has the same knife she used on Bill. She says she didn't have it in the doctor's parking lot. But it's ready for me now."

"Oh, man." Larry sighed. He squeezed my hand again and held on to it. "She's crazy."

"Yes, she's crazy," I agreed. "She's crazy, and she wants to kill me."

Larry motioned to the movie theater. "Are you sure you want to see a movie tonight?"

"Yes. Let's go in," I said, reaching for the door handle. "It will take my mind off Honey."

I hoped that was true.

But it didn't work.

I stared at the movie screen for two hours and thought about Honey. Again and again, I pictured her leaping out at me from behind my car. I heard her furious cries of hatred.

And I pictured her hands in my hair, grasping my head, slamming my face to the hard pavement. Slamming me . . . slamming me . . .

"How did you like it?" Larry asked as we made our way up the aisle.

I blinked and gazed at him blankly. "It was pretty good," I said. I didn't want to admit that I hadn't paid attention to a single minute of it.

"Did you like it when the first volcano erupted?" Larry asked.

"Uh . . . yeah. That was cool," I muttered.

The theater was full. It took us a long time to

walk to the exit. A woman dropped her bag and everything spilled out. She bent over to pick it all up, blocking the whole aisle.

Leaning against Larry, I stopped short.

And felt a hard bump from behind.

"Oh!" I cried out as a sharp blade poked into my back.

"No!" Then the pain shot through my body, and I began to scream.

chapter

25

"Sorry," a girl's voice behind me said.

I whirled around, gasping, my heart pounding.

And gaped at a tall, brown-haired girl in a tan raincoat. She held up a black umbrella. "Sorry," she repeated. "I didn't mean to stab you with this. I tripped."

I pressed my hand over my mouth. My whole body was trembling. People were staring at me, startled by my shrill scream.

"Are you okay?" the girl asked. "Did I hurt you? You screamed—"

"No. I'm fine," I choked out. "Sorry."

I turned back to Larry, who stared at me with concern. "Becka—you scared me to death. I thought—"

"Sorry. Sorry. Sorry," I repeated, my heart still racing.

The aisle finally cleared. Larry put his arm around my shoulders and helped guide me to the doors.

Outside, the rain had stopped but the sidewalks were puddled, and the air felt cold and wet. Car headlights made the puddles glow, and for a moment, I felt as if I were walking on the moon.

Crazy thoughts.

"You're still trembling," Larry said.

"I—I can't calm down," I confessed. "Thanks for being so understanding. When I screamed back there, you must have thought I was totally nuts."

He shrugged. "I didn't know what to think." He pulled his car keys from his jeans pocket. "Want to get some coffee or something to eat? Or should I take you home?"

"Coffee sounds good," I said, forcing a smile. "Something hot might calm me down."

We drove through town. I decided I had to stop being so depressed, so frightened.

Cheer up, Becka, I ordered myself. Give Larry a break.

I turned on the radio and cranked it up really loud. "Remember this song?" I cried. "We used to play it over and over last summer."

I tried singing along with it. But Larry didn't join in. He stared silently into the windshield, his lips pressed together, a tense, thoughtful expression on his face.

So I stopped singing and slumped down in my seat, staring out at the passing buildings. "What are you thinking about?" I asked, shouting over the music.

"Not much," he replied, braking for a red light.

We stopped at the Star Diner out on the Old Mill Road. It's a long, narrow building built to look like an old diner from the 1930s or 1940s. Lots of chrome and neon.

It was pretty crowded. Mostly college students from the Middle College, high school kids, and a few blue-uniformed workers at the counter, leaning over white mugs of coffee, getting ready to head to their night-shift jobs.

Larry and I slid into an aqua-colored vinyl booth near the back. "They have great fries here," Larry announced.

I laughed. "That's what you said the last time we were here."

He looked hurt. "Well, it's true. I wouldn't say it if it wasn't true."

Larry said something else after that. But I didn't hear him.

I was staring down the aisle of the long, narrow diner.

Staring as a girl approached us, moving fast.

Honey!

Running toward me, her knife gleaming . . . gleaming so brightly . . . raised in front of her.

chapter
26

I tried to jump up. To dive from the booth.

No time. No time.

She was coming too fast.

I screamed. And leapt up. Bumped the table hard. Sent the salt and pepper shakers and the metal napkin dispenser toppling to the floor.

Trapped. I was trapped.

"Becka—?" I saw Larry's face fill with alarm. He turned to see where I was staring.

Staring in terror at Honey.

No.

Not Honey.

Not Honey?

I blinked. Blinked again.

And stared at the copper-haired waitress. The waitress, hurrying down the aisle, carrying a steak knife. She gave it to a man in the next booth. Then she turned to me. "Are you okay?"

"No. I . . . uh . . ." I was trying to stand, caught between the table and the vinyl seat. *"I'm not okay!"* I screeched.

I don't know where those words came from.

But I couldn't hold them in.

I couldn't hold back the screams that tore from my throat.

"I'm not okay! She's crazy! She's crazy!" I shrieked.

I caught Larry's startled gasp.

I saw people turning, saw them staring at me, in fear, in confusion.

I saw them all. And I saw myself. As if I were standing outside the booth, watching me tug at my hair with both hands and scream, scream until my throat was raw.

"I'm not okay! She's crazy! She's crazy—and she's going to kill me!"

"But I didn't *do* anything!" the waitress cried, her face bright red.

She thought I was talking about her.

I wanted to stop screaming. I wanted to tell her it wasn't her fault. But how could I?

The screams just wouldn't stop.

And then suddenly, there were hands on my shoulders. And hands at my waist. Someone was pulling me gently from the booth. Someone was leading me down the long aisle.

I saw concerned faces. Saw people staring at me. The blue-uniformed workers at the counter turned and followed me with their eyes as I was led past.

And then I was standing in the parking lot beside

Larry. The wet asphalt gleamed under the glow of the streetlamps. Everything appeared glistening and wet.

The whole world—the trees, the buildings, the cars, the streets—all throbbed. Pulsed and throbbed, as if they had all come alive.

Larry had his arm around me. He led me to the Range Rover and held open the door.

I wasn't screaming anymore, but I couldn't stop shivering.

And I couldn't stop the throbbing. Why was everything bubbling and quivering?

I shut my eyes, forcing it all away, out of sight.

I heard the engine cough and start up. Felt the hum of the big car as we backed out of the parking space and turned onto Old Mill Road.

"Are you feeling better?" Larry's voice seemed so far away. Miles away.

I didn't answer. I kept my eyes tightly shut. I had to stop the pulsing. I had to stop the wet throbbing I saw everywhere.

"Are your parents home? Do you want to call your doctor?"

Larry's questions from so far, far away.

Too far away to answer him. My throat ached from screaming. I knew he'd never hear my reply.

How long did it take to drive home?

I'm not sure. When I opened my eyes, we were pulling up my driveway. The porch light glowed brightly. But the rest of the house was dark.

"My parents went out," I remembered. I turned to Larry. I could see the concern on his face, his eyes narrowed and tense. He gazed at me as if he'd never really seen me before.

"Shall I come in with you?" he asked. "Do you want me to stay until they get home?"

"No," I told him, reaching for the door handle. "I'm feeling better. A lot better."

"I could stay with you," he offered. "It's no problem. Really."

He was being sweet. But I wanted to be alone now. I couldn't take much more of his concerned looks, his worried, probing eyes.

I had to get away from everything and everyone—including Larry.

"I'm going right to sleep," I said, pushing open the door and hopping down. "I'm going to tuck myself in, pull the covers up over my head, and sleep safe and sound."

I tried to smile. But my lips and chin were trembling too hard. So I made a joke instead: "Hey—we'll have to do this again sometime."

He didn't laugh.

I think maybe he'd had his fill of being with a crazy girl. He'd had enough screaming and hysterics for one night.

"Call me tomorrow?" I asked in a tiny voice.

Without giving him a chance to answer, I turned and ran to the house. He waited till I had the front door open. Then the headlights washed over me as he backed out of the drive and sped away.

I stepped into the warm darkness of the house. I took a long, deep breath. Roast chicken smells from dinner lingered in the air.

I closed the door behind me and locked it. Then I stood in the front entryway, breathing deeply, trying to calm myself, waiting for my eyes to adjust to the blue darkness.

I didn't want to turn on any lights. I didn't want to see anything. Pale light from the porch lamp poured in through the tiny glass squares in the top of the front door.

Shapes of furniture came into view. I could see the stairway against the wall.

I made my way over to it, spread my hand over the warm wood of the banister, and pulled myself up the stairs. The upstairs landing was even darker than downstairs. But my room was the first door on the left.

I stepped inside and shut the door. Gray light poured in from the window. The curtains flapped noisily, flying into the room like two ghosts. I hadn't meant to leave the window open. Now it was cold in my room, and damp.

Shivering, I shut the window. Then I pulled off my sweater and corduroy slacks, letting them fall to the floor. I climbed into bed without changing into my nightshirt.

I suddenly felt so tired, so completely drained.

I needed to sleep.

I needed to get warm and cozy under my blankets and heavy quilt.

I lifted the quilt and slid beneath it. I started to settle in.

So happy . . . So happy at last. Safe and sound . . .

"Oh—"

No. Please—no.

Something wet on my back.

Something warm and wet.

The bed. My sheets. Wet . . . and squishy.

"Ohhhhh—"

What happened? What was in my bed?

I struggled to pull myself up. My muscles didn't want to cooperate. I felt sick. My stomach churned. My throat tightened with nausea.

But somehow I managed to climb out. Out of the warm, wet mess. I shoved the blankets away. Stumbled over them as I crossed the dark room.

My hand fumbled for the light switch. Here it is. Yes. Yes. I clicked it on.

And blinked in horror at my bed.

At the red . . . the blood . . . My sheets soaked in blood.

It all went in and out of focus. A red blur at first. And then I saw it so clearly.

My sheets were slashed. Cut to shreds. And soaked in blood.

Dark, red-brown blood.

Bloodstains smeared the wall. A brown handprint glared out at me from the yellow wallpaper behind the headboard.

I let out a low moan and pressed my hands against the sides of my face.

The room went in and out of focus again.

I felt dizzy. The dark red washed over me, like a tall, overpowering ocean wave.

I staggered back—and glimpsed my mirror.

The mirror over my dresser had words scrawled over it. Words in ugly, red block letters:

THIS IS U

Scrawled on my dresser mirror in blood.

THIS IS U

I spun away from the ugly sight. Spun and saw my bed, dripping with blood, the sheets slashed and torn.

THIS IS U

Pressing my hands against my cheeks, I tossed back my head and let out a scream of anger, of horror.

"She was in my house!" I wailed. "Honey was in my house!"

I turned again, my whole body trembling, my head about to explode with rage.

I heard a soft *creak*.

And I saw the bedroom door start to swing open.

She's still here, I realized.

She must have been hiding in the hall.

Honey is still in the house.

And now I'm trapped in here with her.

The door swung all the way open.

"Please—!" I begged. *"Please—don't kill me!"*

chapter

27

"Please—" I murmured, backing away from the door.

Mom's worried face poked into the open doorway. Dad stood right behind her.

"Becka—what's wrong?" Mom asked, her eyes studying me.

Dad pushed past her into my bedroom. His mouth dropped open in shock. "What's *happened* in here?" he cried.

I dove across the room. I threw my arms around Dad and held on to him. "She was in my house!" I shrieked. "She was in my house!"

My parents tried to calm me down. They gave me the pills that Dr. Perlberg had prescribed. They sat close beside me on the couch in the den, and we talked quietly for nearly an hour.

But I couldn't calm down. And I couldn't get to sleep.

I had to sleep on the uncomfortable old cot in the guest room. I stared up at the ceiling all night, listening to the creaks and groans of the house. Listening for footsteps in the hall. Honey's footsteps.

Somewhere around three in the morning, I climbed out of the cot and went to the window. A thick fog had settled over the ground. But through the fog I could see a square of light from the side of Mr. Perkins's house next door.

Is someone awake in there? I wondered, feeling my muscles tense. Is it Honey? Is she next door?

I stayed home from school the next morning. I just couldn't face it. I felt shaken and exhausted.

The police had come early in the morning to check out my room. They tsk-tsked and muttered to themselves and scribbled on their little pads.

One of the officers told me to stay calm.

But what kind of help was that?

"Honey was in my house," I told him shrilly, unable to keep my body from trembling. "In my house! In my house!"

Mom led me to the kitchen for breakfast. But my stomach was a tight knot. I couldn't choke the cornflakes down.

So I stayed home. I was so exhausted, I fell asleep on the den couch with the TV on. I slept most of the day.

Trish and Lilah stopped by that night to see how I was and to bring me the homework. While they were there, Mom decided to run out to the store.

She didn't want to leave me alone, but my friends were with me. And my dad would be home in a little while.

After Mom left, Trish wanted to see my room. But I told her it was too upsetting.

"How did she get in the house?" I asked. I wrapped my arms tightly around myself, as if shielding myself. "How did Honey get in? Now I don't feel safe in my own house. I have to sleep in the guest room. Every time I pass my room, I picture all the blood, the shredded sheets, those words scrawled on my mirror."

"Do you want to come stay with me for a while?" Trish offered.

"You could stay with me," Lilah chimed in. "We've got plenty of room since my brother left for college."

I shook my head. "That's really nice of you," I told them. "But Mom and Dad want me to keep close to home. I think they're worried that . . . that I'm going to totally freak out from all this." And then I added softly, "Like last year."

My friends didn't stay long. They saw that they couldn't cheer me up. It was nice of them to come by. But there really wasn't very much they could do for me. Lilah offered to stay until my dad got home, but I told her not to bother. I knew Dad would show up in a minute.

After Trish and Lilah left, I tried to get through some of the homework. But my mind kept wandering.

For some reason, I found myself thinking about Pinky, a miniature poodle we owned when I was a little girl. Pinky was run over by a car just before my seventh birthday.

I hadn't thought about Pinky in years. I don't know what made me think of him now.

I guess maybe I felt as if I had been run over. I felt as if I had been a hit-and-run victim too.

My dad still wasn't home. I wondered why he was so late. Mom had written his office phone number on a scrap of paper for me. Should I call to see if he was still there?

I kept glancing at the phone number, written in my mother's perfect little printing.

When the phone rang, I nearly jumped out of my skin.

I let it ring and ring.

I didn't want to pick it up. I didn't want to hear any more of Honey's whispered threats.

But then I decided it might be Dad. And if I didn't answer, he'd get really worried.

So I picked up the phone and pressed it to my ear. "Hello?"

"It was so *easy* to get into your house," the whispered voice rasped. "Wait for me, Becka. Your best friend is coming over again tonight. Tonight's the night, Becka. Wait for your best friend."

I tossed the phone to the floor.

And leapt to my feet. The blood pounded in my temples. I could still hear that evil, hoarse whisper ringing in my ears.

"No!" I cried out loud. "No! I can't stay here!"

I had to get out of the house. Honey was coming. She was coming to kill me.

She could be here any second! I told myself. Any second.

If she's right next door . . .

I grabbed my jacket. And hurried down the stairs, taking them two at a time.

"I can't stay here," I murmured out loud. "Can't stay. Can't stay. If she finds me here, she'll *kill* me!"

Where should I go?

Where?

I couldn't think. I couldn't think at all.

I just knew I had to get away.

I hurtled to the front door. Grabbed the doorknob. Turned it. Started to pull open the door.

And someone knocked on the other side.

chapter
28

Too late.

Too late.

The door swung open.

And I gaped in shock at the figure on the front stoop.

"Bill!" I cried. "What are *you* doing here?"

He opened his mouth to answer. But I didn't give him a chance.

"Help me!" I cried. "I've got to get *away* from here!"

"Becka—" he started. "What's wrong? I came over to talk to you. I thought—"

"Honey is coming!" I shrieked. My eyes went to the house next door, dark against the night sky. "She's coming to kill me! I've got to go!"

"I have my car," Bill said. He pointed to the blue Taurus in the driveway. "I'll take you somewhere safe."

His eyes flashed. "I know. Remember my uncle's cabin back in the Fear Street Woods? You'll be safe there. And you can call the police."

I gazed at the car, then back up at the Perkins house. "Okay," I agreed. "Please—let's hurry."

I reached to pull the front door closed—and the phone rang inside the house. I stopped with my hand on the doorknob.

"Are you going to answer that?" Bill asked.

"I'd better," I replied. "It might be Mom and Dad."

I hurried to the phone. "Hello?"

"Hi, it's me." Lilah.

"I can't talk now!" I told her breathlessly. "Honey is coming to kill me. Bill is here. I'm going to hide at his uncle's cabin in the Fear Street Woods. I'll call you when I get there."

Lilah started to reply. But I hung up the phone. Then I ran out to Bill. "Hurry. Let's go!"

We jumped into his car. He started the engine and we began to back down the driveway.

But we didn't make it to the street.

Bright headlights swept over us.

A car pulled into the drive behind us. Blocking us. Blocking my escape.

"It's Honey!" I moaned. "She's here."

chapter

29

I reached for the door handle.

My only hope was to jump out of the car and run.

I pushed open the door.

And saw the other car back up.

It backed into the street—and roared off in the direction it had come.

"It isn't Honey," Bill said. He reached across me and pulled my door shut. "Just someone turning around."

I let out a long sigh. My heart was pounding so hard, I thought my chest might explode.

I shut my eyes as we pulled away. I took a deep breath and held it, trying to calm myself.

I felt Bill's hand squeeze mine. "You're okay now," he said softly.

I opened my eyes. "Why did you come over tonight?" I asked.

Bill shrugged, his eyes on the road ahead. "I thought maybe we could talk."

"Bill—" I started.

But he squeezed my hand again. "The main thing is to get you somewhere safe and sound," he said.

As I stared at him, a wave of tenderness rolled over me. I suddenly remembered how much I used to care about him, how important he had been in my life.

Before . . .

Before Honey ruined everything.

I was still thinking about the way Bill and I cared about each other when we pulled up to his uncle's little cabin. I stepped out of the car. My shoes sank into the soft mud of the front walk.

"Dark back here," Bill muttered. He hurried up to the front door, digging in his jeans pocket for the key.

A gust of wind made the trees whisper. Dry leaves fell all around us, like a silent storm.

I searched for the moon. But it was hidden behind the tall trees. Somewhere in the distance a cat yowled. It sounded so human, it made me shudder.

Bill pushed open the cabin door and motioned for me to come in. He clicked on a ceiling light, and pale, orange light washed over the small front room.

I stepped inside, expecting it to be as cold as outdoors. But to my surprise, it felt warm and cozy. A sweet, tangy aroma greeted me, the smell of a long-burned-out fire in the brick fireplace.

I gazed around the cabin, remembering it well.

THE BEST FRIEND 2

The ratty old couch. The armchair with one arm loose. The pile of old *Sports Illustrated*s stacked beside the fireplace.

When we were going together, Bill and I came here several times to be alone, to get away from the rest of the world.

"Take off your coat," Bill said. "Make yourself comfortable. The phone is over there— remember?" He pointed to the black wall phone beside the faded painting of flamingos. Then he started toward the back.

"Wh-where are you going?" I stammered.

"I think there's some firewood behind the cabin," he replied. "Maybe we can have a fire." He disappeared into the dark back of the cabin. A few seconds later, I heard the back door slam.

I'd better call the police, I decided. I have to tell them that Honey is coming to my house.

I crossed the room and reached for the phone.

It rang, making me cry out in surprise. Who could be calling here? I grabbed up the receiver. "Hello?"

"Becka—you got there!" It was Lilah, sounding very excited.

"Lilah—what's wrong?" I asked.

"You didn't give me a chance to tell you why I called before," she replied. Her voice sounded tinny and far away in the old wall phone.

"What—?" I started.

"Didn't you see the news?" Lilah cried. "Honey was arrested. They caught her upstate. Two days ago."

"Huh?" A stunned gasp escaped my throat.

"She wouldn't give the police her name," Lilah

139

continued. "So they couldn't release the news. The local police didn't even know she'd been caught."

"But—when?" I choked out. "When—?"

"It must have been the day after she beat you up in the parking lot," Lilah replied. "They caught her that night robbing a store upstate. They've been holding her for days!"

"But—but—" I sputtered.

My mind was spinning from the news. I leaned against the cabin wall to steady myself.

"But—if Honey was caught, who slashed my bed?" I cried into the phone. "Who smeared the blood all over my room? And who called me tonight?"

I raised my eyes as Bill stepped back into the room. He had the strangest look on his face.

So hard. So cold . . .

"Put down the phone, Becka," he ordered through clenched teeth. "Put it down—now."

chapter 30

I froze with the phone receiver in my
hand, staring at him. At his clenched fists. At his
dark eyes, narrowed in anger.

I'm in danger, I realized.

I'm in real danger here.

"Put it down, Becka," Bill repeated in a hard,
angry voice I didn't even recognize.

I ignored him. I turned away from him. And
frantically started to push 911.

With an angry cry, he hurtled across the room,
bumping the old armchair hard with one knee as he
came.

"Bill—no!" I cried as he roared up to me, hands
raised.

I ducked away, thinking he was going to grab me.

But he grabbed the phone instead. Grabbed it
with both hands. And ripped it off the wall.

Breathing hard, he heaved it across the cabin. It

hit the wall above the fireplace and clattered to the wooden floor.

He turned to me, his chest heaving, struggling to catch his breath.

I tried to back away. But I was already up against the wall.

"Bill—why?" I managed to cry out.

A cold sneer curled his lips. "Why? Becka, you should know why," he seethed.

I stared wide-eyed at him. "You?" I cried. *"You* have been the one calling me? *You* sneaked into my house and—and—"

"Not me," Bill replied, still sneering. "Not me, Becka."

My mind swirled with confusion. "Then who—?" I started.

I didn't finish my question.

I saw something move at the back of the cabin.

A girl stepped slowly into the light, her arms crossed tightly in front of her.

"You?" I shrieked. "What are *you* doing here?"

chapter

31

She glared angrily across the cabin at me. "Why shouldn't I be here?" Trish demanded. "I'm your best friend—aren't I?"

"But, Trish—" I started. "I don't understand. You *are* my best friend! So why—?"

Her face went white. Her chin trembled as she lowered her hands, clenching them into tight fists. "You're no friend of mine!" she declared nastily. "I've hated you, Becka, ever since my party last year," Trish continued. Her eyes burned furiously into mine. She didn't blink. "I was pushed down the stairs and broke my neck—remember?" she cried.

"Of course I remember," I shot back. "But why—?"

"Where were you after that, Becka?" Trish demanded. "I was in the hospital for so long. But where were *you?* You didn't come to see me—did you?" she accused.

"I couldn't," I broke in. "I explained to you, Trish. I couldn't."

"You hardly came to see me at all," Trish continued bitterly. "Sure you couldn't. You couldn't because you were so wrapped up in yourself. You only cared about taking care of yourself, Becka."

"That isn't fair!" I protested.

But Trish wasn't listening to me. She turned to Bill. "He came to see me every day," she said, her expression softening. "Bill was so sweet. So wonderful. And he was so *hurt* by you."

"Now, wait—" I pleaded.

"You dumped us both!" Trish screamed. She shook her fist at me. "Bill and I—we were your friends—your *real* friends. But you dumped us both. Why? Why? Because you only care about yourself!"

"That's not fair!" I cried again, taking a step toward her. "Listen to me, Trish."

"You only care about yourself," Trish repeated bitterly. "You don't have time for friends. Because *you* are your only friend, Becka."

A single tear slid down her pale, white cheek. "You hurt us both," she accused in a trembling voice. "We cared about you—and you threw us away like trash. But I didn't forget you—*friend.*" She uttered the word as if it were something ugly and disgusting.

"Look," Trish ordered. "Look, *friend.* I brought the shiny present I promised you over the phone."

She raised a large kitchen knife in front of her.

The big blade flashed in the orange light from the ceiling.

"Hey—what are you *doing?*" Bill demanded shrilly, moving toward Trish. "You—you didn't say anything about a knife. You promised me you only wanted to scare her!"

Bill dove for her.

Trish slid past him.

She raised the knife above her head.

Before I could move—before I could even scream—she brought it down hard.

chapter

32

"Noooooooooo!" A horrified wail escaped my lips.

Trish swung the knife down—as Bill dove between us to stop her.

And she swung the blade deep into his chest.

His eyes bulged in pain. He uttered a choked cry. And slumped in a heap to the cabin floor.

"Look what you did!" Trish shrieked at the top of her lungs. "Look what you did, Becka! Look what you did! You stabbed him again! You stabbed him again!"

"No—Trish! Listen to me!" I pleaded, my eyes on Bill's unmoving body. On the bright red blood that puddled out over the wooden floor.

But Trish raised the bloodstained knife and moved toward me again.

I stared in horror as she approached.

I *am* my own best friend! I told myself. I have to be strong. I *have* to be my own best friend now.

Somehow that thought gave me new strength.

With a hideous animal cry, Trish plunged the knife at my chest.

But as she swung down, I grabbed the handle. Wrestled both hands around it.

"Nooooo!" Trish protested.

We struggled for a moment. Staring into each other's eyes.

Gasping for breath, I slid the knife from her hands.

Turned the handle.

Pressed the blade to her throat.

Pressed it against her pale skin until a tiny line of red trickled down.

She uttered a cry of pain. Stopped struggling.

And backed away, holding her neck. Pressing her hands against the small cut.

I stood trembling, the knife in both hands.

And heard the high wail of sirens in the distance.

And knew that Lilah had called the police.

Trish cowered in the corner, holding her throat.

I moved over to Bill.

He lay on his back, his head against the wall. A bright circle of blood spread over the front of his shirt. He gazed up at me, blinking hard from the pain, one hand spread over the wound.

"Hold on, Bill," I told him. "Hold on."

I knelt down beside him. "I won't forget you this

147

time," I told him. "I'll be a good friend. I promise."

The sirens grew louder.

I reached down and he grabbed my hand.

I held on to it, held it, held it tightly. "I'll be your friend, Bill," I whispered. "I'll be a good friend. I promise."

About the Author

R.L. Stine is the best-selling author in America. He has written more than one hundred scary books for young people, all of them bestsellers.

His series include *Fear Street, Ghosts of Fear Street* and the *Fear Street Sagas*.

Bob grew up in Columbus, Ohio. Today he lives in New York City with his wife, Jane, his teenage son, Matt, and his dog, Nadine.

THE NIGHTMARES NEVER END . . . WHEN YOU VISIT

Next . . .

TRAPPED

(Coming mid-November 1997)

There's an old story about the tunnels under Shadyside High. Kids used to party down there, back in the sixties. Until something horrible happened. Something that left a lot of people dead.

It's just a story. Elaine knows there's nothing to be afraid of. And exploring the tunnels is more fun than being stuck in Saturday detention.

Besides, it's not as if anything could still be *alive* down there . . . right?

R.L. STINE'S
GHOSTS OF FEAR STREET ®

FEAR STREET®

THE BEST FRIEND
BEST FRIENDS...TO THE END!

Who is Honey Perkins? She's been telling everyone in Shadyside that she's Becka Norwood's best friend. But Becka's sure she's never met Honey before.

Does Honey just want a friend?
Or does she want more—*much* more!

THE BEST FRIEND 2
THE BOOK *YOU* DEMANDED!

In *The Best Friend*, Honey Perkins got away with murder. Now, R.L. Stine has chosen a winner from a nationwide contest asking readers, "What Should Happen to Honey?"

Honey is back. And this time she won't stop—
until Becka is dead.

By

R.L. Stine

POCKET
BOOKS

Available from Archway Paperbacks
Published by Pocket Books

1441

When the cheers turn to screams...

CHEERLEADERS

The First Evil
75117-4/$3.99

The Second Evil
75118-2/$3.99

The Third Evil
75119-0/$3.99

**Available from Archway Paperbacks
Published by Pocket Books**

Simon & Schuster Mail Order
200 Old Tappan Rd., Old Tappan, N.J. 07675
Please send me the books I have checked above. I am enclosing $_____ (please add $0.75 to cover the postage
and handling for each order. Please add appropriate sales tax). Send check or money order—no cash or C.O.D.'s
please. Allow up to six weeks for delivery. For purchase over $10.00 you may use VISA: card number, expiration
date and customer signature must be included.

Name _____

Address _____

City _____ State/Zip _____

VISA Card # _____ Exp.Date _____

Signature _____ 854